# CATAPULT

by

J.C. BENTHIN

This book is a work of fiction. Names, characters, places and incidents either are productions of the author's imagination or used fictitiously. Any resemblance to actual events or locals or persons, living or eat is entirely coincidental.



Designed by David Provolo

Manufactured in the United States of America

ISBN: 9781093513820

Independently published

*For Lena*

*For your constant encouragement*

# CHAPTER 01

*WHAM!*

Kingston's motorcycle slid to an abrupt stop on the pavement. His head snapped up to view an accident still in progress. It happened in seconds even though it felt like slow motion. He watched as a sedan slammed into the front of a van. The car rotated four times in the center of the road, hopped the curb, and rammed directly into a streetlight, sending sparks in all directions. The van rolled sluggishly forward then halted on the opposite side of the road. All was quiet until Kingston commanded his Bluetooth-enabled helmet to dial 911. He parked and hopped off his bike in one smooth movement. His chest tightened as he walked over to the sedan.

A woman's voice clucked through the built-in speaker in his helmet. "Nine-one-one, what's your emergency?"

He shivered. The December night was colder than normal around the outskirts of downtown Oakland. He reluctantly flipped up the visor on his helmet and checked the street signs. "There's been an accident on Seventh and Adeline."

"Were you involved in it, sir?"

"No," said Kingston as he approached the first car.

"Can you describe the vehicles that were involved?"

"A silver sedan and a white van."

"Is anybody hurt, sir?"

"Not sure. Let me check."

As Kingston reached the first car, he found a frail elderly woman with white-blue hair who looked as though she could barely see over the steering wheel. The engine was whining, so Kingston got into the passenger side and turned off the car. She was unconscious, breathing and leaning forward on an airbag. A small trickle of blood was coming out of her nose. She was probably around his grandfather Papa Juan's age, early seventies. She had a nice face just like his Nana. At least that's what his five-year-old memory of his grandmother told him.

"Sir, are you still on the line?"

"Yeah, an older lady is hurt pretty bad. Want me to get her out?"

Kingston exited the passenger side and walked to the driver's side, but the operator's voice stopped his hand before he reached the driver's-side door. "Is the car smoking or on fire?"

"No," he replied.

"Then wait for the paramedics to arrive. What about the other vehicle?"

"Hold on, checking..."

Kingston strode across the cold, damp street to find no driver for the windowless van. The keys were still in the ignition, slightly swinging back and forth.

"Not sure where the driver is."

"Ambulance is en route. Should arrive in five minutes," said the operator. "Sir, can you stay with the vehicles until the police arrive?"

"Yeah," said Kingston, even though his answer should've been no since he was going to be late again to his graveyard shift as a part-time security officer at the Port of Oakland.

"Your name, please?"

"Kingston Rais."

After the operator hung up, Kingston stepped to the front of the van and leaned on the hood then commanded his phone to dial his coworker Rustic. "Hey. You want the good news or the bad news?"

"Wild guess, you're gonna be late, again," Rustic said.

"Yeah, a little. Could you cover?"

"Probably. Everything okay?"

"Yep, I'm fine. But this old lady isn't. Not sure if she should've been driv—"

*CLANG!*

Kingston's breath quickened. He stood up and walked around the vehicle to see the back of a large, beefy man with a gun in his hand. Kingston quickly took cover and flattened himself against the side of the van. He heard the man huffing loudly and rattling off expletives as he stomped across the street to the sedan.

He crouched down by the bumper and caught a glimpse of the red-faced man using the barrel of the gun to move the head of the lady.

"Oh boy," Kingston wheezed out.

"What?" Rustic asked.

"I found the other driver. Gotta go."

"King—"

Kingston hung up. His thoughts went wild. Adrenaline rushed through his body like a wildfire. What could he do? How could he save this lady? He pushed down a cough. He didn't have time for an asthma attack. He ripped the inhaler out of his pocket and sucked in the medicated air ferociously.

Kingston then realized, as he stuffed his inhaler back in his pocket, he did have something. He made his way around to the driver's side of the van and quietly opened the door, then he slid into the driver's seat. He turned on the ignition, yanked the gearshift into drive, and slammed his foot down on the accelerator. The van lurched forward, sputtered, and picked up speed. It was no Lamborghini, but it was moving.

The driver of the van yelled and clumsily started running after it. There was no way that he would catch the van on foot. The man lost steam and started shooting at the van. A bullet whizzed and clanked against the back door. Kingston ducked down and kept the steering wheel straight, popping up only to make sure he wasn't going to hit anything. Sirens wailed in the distance, sending the message that help was on the way. Kingston glanced at the rearview mirror and caught a glimpse of the guy running away, down another block.

"Call Rustic," Kingston commanded his phone.

The line barely rang once before Rustic answered. "What is—"

Kingston cut him off. "Hey, sorry. Had to deal with the other driver."

"You trying to give me a full-blown heart attack?" Rustic grumbled out.

"I'll tell you the whole story when I get to work."

Rustic let out a slow sigh and said, "Fine. Hurry it up."

"All right. See you in a few," Kingston said as he parked the van behind the lady's car and hopped out just as the police and paramedics arrived.

Kingston pulled off his helmet and rattled off all the details to the police. He was good at seeing the details. "He was a heavy man, two hundred eighty pounds or so," Kingston said.

"And wore a white, ripped T-shirt and black jeans. He had a mustache and short-cropped hair. The man took off running down Magnolia and couldn't have made it too far. Looks like the van is full of stolen electronics."

Once he'd made his statement and the elderly lady was loaded into the ambulance, Kingston put on his helmet and hopped back onto his motorcycle.

By the time Kingston rolled into the Port of Oakland, he was fifty minutes late. He parked next to a covered container that served as the security office. The hum of thirty-five different screens marking every angle of the port greeted his eyes.

Rustic appeared in his line of sight by stretching his wiry arms up. His dark uniform was always baggy and wrinkled. His salt-and-pepper hair was pressed down on his head where he normally wore his lucky ball cap. He always had a mischievous grin on his face. Rustic may not look like much, but he was fast and could outmaneuver anyone. He'd been working security at the port for over twenty years, right after he finished his active duty with the military as a member of a special ops team inside the Navy SEALs.

He wished he could follow in Rustic's footsteps. Unfortunately, his "condition" disqualified him. However, Rustic had trained Kingston how to think on his feet and use his strengths to his advantage.

"It's about time your butt got here," said Rustic.

Kingston half smiled as he pushed his hand back through his dark, thick hair, shoving a lock behind his ear. He spilled out a quick version of what happened and ended with "Can you believe that he was stupid enough to shoot at his own van?"

"I don't remember you being bulletproof. Trust me, it hurts

to get shot. Headline: YOU COULD DIE. You gotta be more careful," exclaimed Rustic.

"I can't help it. I can't just pass by. I'd regret it."

"Regret is better than being in the grave. What's wrong with you, son? It's like you got some sort of inner radar that leads you to every person on the planet who's in distress," poked Rustic.

Kingston shrugged and said, "At least it's exciting."

Rustic smiled and wagged his finger. "Death's not that exciting."

Kingston smirked as he scanned his key card into the computer indicating that he had begun his evening shift. "That would be more entertaining than watching containers just sit there."

Rustic reached over and squeezed Kingston's shoulder then lit up a cigarette as he burst out the door. "Have a great night, King Rais!"

"Not sure if you know this, but those things cause cancer," Kingston replied, pointing at the cigarette.

"You know, nowadays everything does. I want to enjoy my life, not follow their rules," Rustic chuckled.

Kingston watched as a legend in his own right walked away. He would never say it out loud, but Rustic was a better dad to him than his own.

Kingston sighed and picked up a rubber band from the pile on the desk. He stretched it out and aimed it at one of the monitors. The rubber band sailed across and hit the screen smack dab in the middle. His old friend, boredom, entered the room. When he was a kid, he didn't think that this would be his future. He always thought he would do something meaningful with his life. But here he was, package delivery boy by day and security guard by night. His dad made it explicitly clear that if he didn't do well in school, then he'd have no future. As hard as he tried, school was never his thing. Truthfully, he had no idea what his thing was. In fact, the only reason that he had this job was because his dad was high up in the port authority. He was fulfilling his dad's unspoken prediction of what a nothing he would become. Nothing his dad was proud of.

The screens flickered. Kingston came back to reality. He grabbed a pair of night-vision goggles and a horse tranquilizer gun that had been left behind from a previous shipment of horses; it'd be the perfect weapon if he needed one. This was his only break from the monotony of the night. Making rounds wasn't really necessary since the entire port was wired with alarms and cameras, but he liked to turn it into a game of sorts. If the head of security or his dad, the director of maritime at the Port of Oakland, caught wind of the fact that he had turned this lame security job into a race against the clock, then he might be in serious trouble. Thankfully, containers don't speak, and Kingston knew exactly when to walk through the security camera feed. At least he could pretend that his life was exciting he thought as he pushed out into the chilly air.

# CHAPTER 02

The air-conditioning in the TV studio made the hairs on Sam Waters's arm stand on end. He normally ran hot and enjoyed the cool air. But today he felt a little under the weather, a little chilled. The television crew scurried around the studio adjusting lights, setting camera angles, and preparing for the taping. This movement all around him almost seemed choreographed as he sat in the make up chair waiting to move to the set.

Sam examined his reflection lit up by the makeup station, his white-silver hair lightly styled and two paper towels sticking out of his shirt like white wings begging him to fly away. He absolutely hated interviews, especially putting makeup all over his face like a suffocating blanket. However, this part of the illusion was critical to keeping appearances well defined in the public eye.

An overenthusiastic young girl in her early twenties appeared in the mirror and said, "Mr. Waters, would you mind taking a seat on set? Ms. Winners will be with you shortly."

Sam pulled his wings off, put on his jacket, and eased out of the chair. He shivered a little. He wondered if he had the flu as he sauntered over to his chair on set and took his place. His eyes focused on the cement floor in response to the bright lights. To the outside world, his persona communicated that he was a successful billionaire who stepped down from his role as CEO of Titanium Fortress Investments and was now doing "foundation" work. It was the perfect cover. No one would suspect that he was secretly creating an elite black ops team to help stop the madness in the world.

Suddenly, Elizabeth Winners, a sharp, put-together woman with a welcoming presence and a quick tongue, appeared in front of him. Her glistening smile was almost as bright as the studio lights. She extended her perfectly manicured hand with confidence and grace, shook and gave a light squeeze before letting go. "Mr. Waters, so glad to have you back this evening."

"Ms. Winners, please call me Sam."

Her laugh, as if on cue, was musical and polite before she got down to business and said, "Sam, we're just going through the usual general questions on what to invest your money in the new year. The segment will air New Year's Eve during the eleven o'clock news hour, barring any national disaster."

"Great."

Her happy, animated face became quickly distraught when she spoke at almost a whisper so that no one could hear. "I'm so sorry to hear about the loss of your wife, Esther. She was such a lovely woman."

Sam quietly responded, "Thank you for your kind words and for the flowers."

Elizabeth took her seat, covered her microphone, and continued to keep her voice low as she pushed one side of her hair behind her shoulder. "It was the least I could do, given all that has happened to you with your son and now your wife. Honestly, I would be a complete wreck if I lost my husband and child. I don't know how you leave the house. "

Sam forced a smile. "Moving forward is the only thing that keeps me sane."

"Good for you."

A brief sound cue played signaling the door to the set was closing and the floor director had entered the room.

"Quiet on the set," the floor director yelled.

Ms. Winners didn't miss a beat. She straightened her back and put on her serious face with a slight smile and looked directly into the lens of the camera. The floor director counted down, "Five, four, three, two..." and signaled a silent one, then pointed at the camera with the red light on.

*Tonight we have with us one of America's iconic businessmen, Sam Waters. He's considered a modern-day Rockefeller and has been at the top of* Forbes *World's Billionaires list for several years now. He came from humble beginnings and became a rising star through the investment banking ranks. Once he established himself, he struck out on his own and built the top investment firm in the world, Titanium Fortress Investments. Recently, he stepped down as CEO and passed the company on to his former COO, Hunter Silas. Now he has focused his energy on philanthropy and giving back.*

*ELIZABETH WINNERS: Mr. Waters, Thanks for joining us tonight.*

*SAM: My pleasure.*

*ELIZABETH WINNERS: How is retirement treating you?*

*SAM: I wouldn't say I—uh—am retired exactly. I like to think of it as shifting roles.*

*ELIZABETH WINNERS: What role are you taking on now?*

*SAM: I'm working at the Jefferson Waters Foundation in honor of the death of my son.*
*ELIZABETH WINNERS: Many of our viewers may remember that terrorist attack in 2005 when three trains were bombed in London. Your son, Jefferson, was on one of those trains?*
*Sam pauses and sips water.*
*SAM: Yes, unfortunately he was. I gave him the gift to travel through Europe as a college graduation present.*
*ELIZABETH WINNERS: Very sad, at such a young age.*
*SAM: Yes, the main goal of the Jefferson Waters Foundation is to help victims' families recover from any and all terrorist attacks.*
*ELIZABETH WINNERS: I'm sure your son would be proud of the work you are doing.*
*SAM: Thank you for saying that.*
*ELIZABETH WINNERS: Now, after the break, I was hoping you could share some of your financial wisdom in this uncertain time.*
*SAM: I would be happy to.*

The director's voice sounded: "And we're clear."

Elizabeth Winners peeked at her phone and said, "Hey, Sam, I've got to return a call. Back in a few."

Sam closed his eyes in an attempt to push away a headache that was forming as he thought about Elizabeth's comment pertaining to uncertain times. Uncertain times was a complete understatement. The world had cracked. Fear underlined freedom. Shootings happened anywhere at any time. Terror attacks were frequent and elaborate, and the government was having a hard time keeping up. Violent acts were happening often at home and abroad, so it almost seemed like the new normal. He never thought that in his lifetime people would be so afraid to go to a concert or a ball game or fly across the country. The fear was palpable.

Then the fear caused people in this country to be divided. Division always produces vulnerability. It wasn't simply one people's group against another. It was even more complicated, with a thread of rage running through the veins of many. It had only worsened since the death of his son, and he couldn't just watch and not do something.

Sam truly believed that it was his duty to protect the blind side—the side that no one saw coming because the governments of the world focused on the bigger attacks. He prided himself in being solution focused, and he now felt like he finally had an answer.

Sure, he had a foundation; at least that's what everyone saw from the outside. Instead of getting lost in the grief over his son, he quietly established a private security company twelve years ago—Platinum Security Group. He worked with the best military minds in the world and had put together several tactical teams to target imminent and hidden threats.

His phone buzzed. He pulled it out of his pocket and read a text from Lincoln.

**Did you get the update?**

Sam paused then responded to Lincoln.

**No. At studio. Will check right now.**

Sam put his phone into his right pocket then reached into his left pocket and pulled out another phone identical to his own. He calmly pressed the side button and immediately all cell phones in the studio lost service. He was completely secure. He opened up the private intranet and saw a video with a short report from Dr. Greystone. He put his earbuds in and watched the video. His shoulders drooped and he sighed. He pressed a button again and all service was restored. He methodically put the secure phone back into his pocket and retrieved the other one.

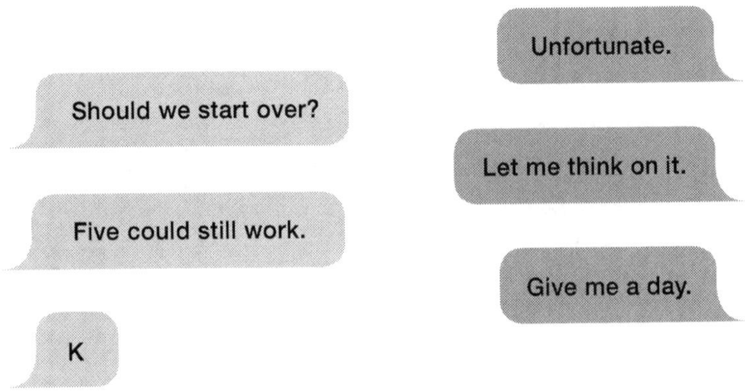


Sam slid his normal phone back into his right pocket, shaking his head. PSG was one year into developing a privatized elite team. They had trained five different teams sanctioned by the government to handle specific off-the-books missions, but this team was different. This team was created to work in the shadows. Three of the six members had been recruited directly out of college and trained to protect, avert, and stop any and all attacks. The other three were pulled from lucrative professional lives. They were young. They were talented. They were hungry. But most of all, they believed in the cause to make the world a safe place once again.

One of the recruits had slid off the rails. Kaj was a re asset. He was sharp, committed, and passionate. It was a the team.

He wasn't sure what his next move should be. He liked even numbers. Lincoln was right, they could make it with five; however, Sam felt he would always wonder how much more they could do with six.

Elizabeth returned to her chair and said, "Are you ready?"

"Yes ma'am," replied Sam.

The director repeated his floor calls and the light turned red on the camera.

*ELIZABETH WINNERS: Our viewers are really interested in what you think they should invest their money in now that we are entering the new year.*

*SAM: Pick long-standing companies, diversify, and save.*

Kingston fidgeted with the rubber band around his wrist on the eve of the new year as he mindlessly stared at the screens in the security office at the Port of Oakland. He was bored out of his mind, not even his vivid imagination could save him from this constant hum of nothing. He swore to himself that this year his resolution would be to do something, anything, other than this.

Kingston's phone whistled. It was a text from his best friend, Cooper.

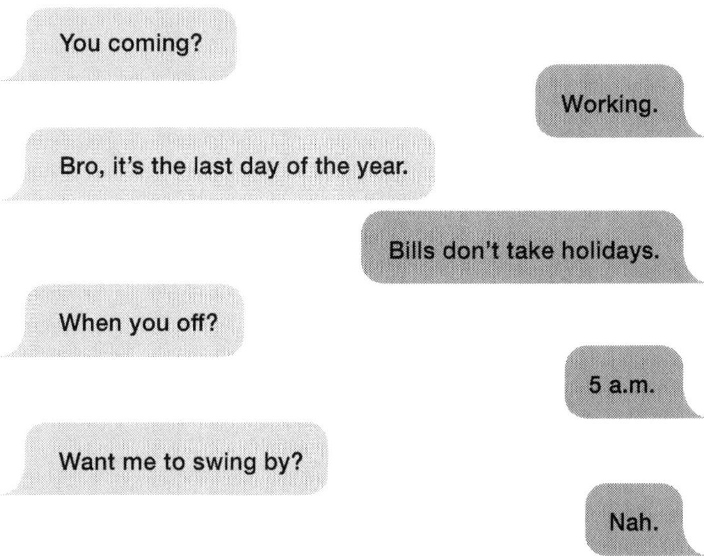

Late lunch on the flip then? On me.

I can do that.

Kingston tossed his phone on the desk. He took the rubber band off his wrist and began stretching it between his thumb and index finger. He then glanced up at the screens and noticed a black car pulling into the dock. It looked like his brother Jude's car. Kingston wondered what his brother was doing here so late? Two minutes later, Jude walked through the door.

Jude studied the camera angles. "One of my guys said that a piece of equipment knocked into camera seventeen, and I wanted to take a look at it."

"The one in the customs area?"

Kingston and Jude cocked their heads sideways at the screen, and the angle did seem to be off slightly.

"Do you want me to call Satco Images to set up a repair?" asked Kingston.

"I should go take a look at it since they won't be out to repair it until after the holiday. See if I can put it back on track. Can you power down the camera so I don't get electrocuted?" asked Jude.

"Can do," Kingston said as he looked at the log to check what containers were there. "Is Grazeco a new company?"

"Yeah, the contract just started, and I want to keep them happy on their first delivery to the Port of Ensenada."

"Fertilizer?"

"A very special mix that keeps the fall armyworm at bay," Jude replied.

Kingston grinned and flipped off the camera. "Betcha it smells real good in there."

"Like a dream. I'll be back in when I'm done," said Jude over his shoulder as he left the office.

Kingston swiveled around in his chair and extended his arms. "Happy New Year to you, bro."

It was hard living in his brother's shadow. Jude was good at everything he did. He was strong academically. He was the captain of his football team. He dated the best-looking girl in high school and college. He graduated with honors. He was a natural-born leader, and everyone liked him.

His brother Jude, or rather the favored one of his family, had recently been promoted from foreman to sales manager for shipping accounts. He had the advantage of understanding how the port worked as well as the ability to charm the clients. It did seem odd that he would visit the port this late, especially on a holiday when he would normally be making a ruckus at the local bar.

Kingston's curiosity was peaked with his brother's surprise visit. It gave him a reason to stretch his legs. He shoved the rubber band in his pocket, put on the night-vision goggles, and grabbed the tranquilizer gun. He stepped out into the cold, brisk air. He huffed warm air on his hands.

He started off jogging on the north side of the port, figuring he'd finish rounds near Jude and see if he needed any help. As he picked up the pace, his mind wandered back to the day of his eighteenth birthday. His dad—er—the director tossed him the security uniform and informed him that since Kingston's grades were "piss-poor" he needed to stop living off his dad's hard-earned money, and come graduation Kingston would be on his own. So, here he was living the nightmare doing exactly the opposite of what he wanted to do.

Several minutes later, Kingston reached the customs area, but Jude had already disappeared. The dock was clear and it was unusually silent. But something felt off. But then again…

He walked back into the office, tossed his gear aside, and studied all the camera feeds. He noticed that camera seventeen was back on and in the right position. He saw nothing out of the ordinary, but his gut still told him something was off. A small red light started blinking on the control panel, followed by a piercing shrill of an alarm. Someone or something had tripped the wire by C gate. The last two times it had been a wounded seagull, but he had to check it out. He moved quickly over to the logs to see what containers were in that location. C-10378 held plastic toys, 79 held electronic bidet toilet seats, 80 a shipment of clothes, 81 some sort of chemical. He checked the license for that one. It was ammonium nitrate fuel oil in crystal form. That was not good, not good at all. Those crystals were used to blow up stuff at quarry mines. He suited up again and took off running.

He was two-aisles away when he heard scraping and muffled voices. Kingston froze. He pulled out his phone and dialed 911 without thinking, without following protocol. He whispered into the phone, "Hi, yes, I'd like to report trespassers down at the Port of Oakland. You better hurry! Don't think they'll be here long."

He hung up as he heard the voice on the other end say, "Please stay where you are, sir, in a safe location."

He crept closer to the voices and he heard a male voice say, "Hurry up! We got about two trips left."

Kingston knew right then and there he had to do something.

He knew that to get a good view without being noticed, he would have to go vertical. He scaled the cold, wet metal. He crawled up on the containers with ease. He had been climbing these containers since he was ten. He soundlessly hopped from one container to the next. Then he focused his night-vision goggles and saw two figures in black unloading a container. He slid down on his stomach and grabbed his tranquilizer gun. He had only one shot. He counted the seconds each time one figure entered and exited the container. He realized he had five seconds to take out both opponents.

He placed the gun down on the roof of the container and set his goggles to act as a scope. His hands were sweating. But it was game time. He felt his chest constrict. Kingston slowed his breathing and peered through the goggles, silently counting the rhythm of their movements. He clenched his hands then uncurled his fingers and allowed his body to slowly melt silently into the moment. He willed his racing heart to beat to a slow bump. He grabbed his inhaler and pressed relief into his lungs.

His mind traveled back to when he turned fifteen and Rustic took him under his wing. He would take Kingston to the gun range and show him how to get into the zone by slowing his breathing, relaxing his muscles, and focusing solely on the target.

One of the men yelled, bringing Kingston back into focus.

The first man clothed in black entered the container. *One.* The second man was returning with his cart. Kingston aimed for his leg. *Two.* He shot the second man, and like a panther, Kingston leapt off the top of the container and swung the door shut as the wounded man yelled to his partner. *Three.* He jammed the tranquilizer gun into the latch of the container, locking it shut. *Four.* He jetted over to the man on the ground and grabbed ahold of his phone before he could alert anyone. *Five.* He sunk to the ground not noticing his bloody hands and feet from the drop. His heartbeat returned so strong in his ears that he barely heard the sirens approaching above the relentless pounding of the first man in the container.

The once quiet night soon turned into a circus. Ten police cars showed up, and four FBI agents and a crime scene unit appeared on scene. They quickly had yellow tape up around the perimeter of the container. Within minutes, both men—one conscious and screaming obscenities, the other still out from the horse-sleeping juice—were cuffed and lying on the ground. The officer in charge thoroughly searched both men for weapons. He removed their jackets, revealing their arms, and Kingston noticed a pronounced lion tattoo on the bigger man's forearm.

A few minutes later, a news truck rolled up and a young redhead popped out of the truck and scurried around asking questions until she reached Kingston.

"Hi, I'm Abi, an intern at KPZX News," she said. "In a few minutes, Elizabeth Winners will be over here to ask you some questions on camera. Is that okay?"

"I don't know if I should…," Kingston replied.

Abi's face pleaded with him. "Please. It's my first night in the field and it would be such a help to me."

Kingston grinned. "All right. I guess it couldn't hurt that much."

"Great! What's your name? First and last? Could you spell your last name for me?"

"Kingston Rais. That's R-A-I-S."

The impeccably dressed blonde, who Kingston assumed to be Elizabeth Winners, appeared alongside Abi. She flashed a smile and extended her hand toward him.

"Hello. You must be Kingston," she said.

Kingston nodded, and before he could get another word out, she took control. The next thing he knew, he was in front of a camera telling his story about taking down two criminals. The well-versed reporter heralded him as a hero for catching a father-and-son duo, Rufus and James McCleary, known for several chemical heists in three different states. They claimed that the contents of the container were stolen from them, and they were simply getting back what rightfully belonged to them. As soon as the camera lights clicked off, Jude rolled up and hopped out of his car in one singular motion. He did not look happy.

"What in the world happened?"

"Not sure. Somehow they got inside the gate," said Kingston.

Jude paused and studied the chaos around them. "You didn't speak to the press, right?"

Kingston avoided looking directly at Jude. "Maybe."

Jude waved his arms around like a maniac and smacked his brother's head as he said, "Have you gone loco in the head? Dad will lose his mind."

"Listen, I stopped the thieves," defended Kingston.

Jude sighed long and shook his head. "Doesn't matter. This incident affects the reputation of the port."

The high that Kingston was riding quickly deflated as he sensed that this would not end well for him. "Did you recheck the container to make sure nothing is missing?" he asked.

"Yep, all the contents are accounted for."

"At least you have that working for you."

Jude then noticed the blood on Kingston's hands. "You better take off. Go get that looked at. I'll run interference with Dad and head of security when they show up."

"What about protocol?" asked Kingston.

"What about it? You've already done enough damage. Besides it'll give Dad a chance to cool down before he takes your head off."

"Thanks, bro."

"Get out of here before I change my mind," Jude said.

Kingston hightailed it out of there knowing that the tsunami named Tomas Rais was headed in his direction, and no matter what, it was going to go down and not end well for him.

# CHAPTER 04

Sam Waters couldn't get to sleep again. The billionaire stared at the ceiling, wishing he could just get some shut-eye. He got out of bed and made his way to the window, where he barely acknowledged the fireworks dotting the San Francisco skyline from his luxury hotel in the Oakland hills.

He knew why he couldn't sleep—he missed the way she breathed when she slept. He missed stealing the covers from her. He missed how she would beg him to retire. He'd tried everything. Sleeping pills didn't work. Strenuous workouts didn't work. Therapy didn't work. Nothing seemed to make the grief go away. There was that saying: "What does it profit a man to gain the world, yet lose his own soul." He felt as though he'd lost a part of his soul when she'd left for good. He had billions, yet no amount of money could've stopped her from dying. There was no profit in that…

The only true solace he found was busying himself in his work, not for the extra dollar, but because his work made him feel alive. He could hear his wife now: "Sam, you need a hobby. Go have some fun. All this work, it's not good for your health." But it was the only thing that seemed to give him any sort of purpose.

He looked over at the pile of folders haphazardly stacked on his desk. They were the top fifty families who had applied to the assistance program from his foundation. His wife had always picked the top fifteen who needed the most assistance and now it was up to him. He had fourteen pretty much locked in, but he still had to decide on the fifteenth. He mindlessly perused each file. The faces started to blur together, and the words turned into mush, each explaining their desperate need for the Jefferson Waters Foundation Fund.

He paused for a second and thought about Jefferson. His one and only son with blazing brown eyes and a curly mop of hair. Sam had to hold himself back from sneaking into his room at night and lopping it all off. But like his hair, his son had his own mind. He wished he could've changed it. He wished he could rewind twelve years and stop Jefferson from going on that trip. He wished he would've given him a car instead. He wondered what his life would be like if that event hadn't occurred. He wondered with that one change would his wife ended up cancer free?

Grief haunted him.

Now with both his wife and son no longer with him, death was his greatest enemy. He was more determined than ever to save many others from suffering unjustly.

It was a hobby at first, but now it was a full-fledged obsession. He wanted to fight the enemy that had taken his son from him. This privatized elite team had yet to have their first real mission. Sam couldn't shake the feeling that they needed one more person to round out the group. He needed someone special to fill that role.

He pushed the folders aside and turned on the TV.

The fireworks had just ended when a breaking news report appeared onscreen.

He sighed and flipped channels on the TV, then landed on the local news as the story of Kingston Rais popped onto the screen with the heading LOCAL HERO.

*ELIZABETH WINNERS: Weren't you afraid?*
*KINGSTON: Yep, but you can't allow fear to keep you from doing the right thing.*

Sam thought for a moment. He said to himself, "Kingston Rais." The team would survive the loss of Kaj, but surviving wasn't a word that Sam accepted in the vocabulary of his life. He wanted the team to be exceptional. This kid could be that solution he was looking for; hopefully, Lincoln felt the same way.

Lincoln, Hunter's son, was one of his accidental recruits. He turned out to be quite the wonder. Lincoln wasn't sure what to do after college and decided to intern for Sam as a personal assistant to get a feel for what a CEO of a major investment company was like. By accident, Lincoln stumbled onto his secret and wanted in. He wore Sam down. Sam had to reveal the existence of the security company to Hunter and then ask him if his son could be a part of it. It was a hard conversation at first, but Hunter came around recognizing that the experience would be useful for Lincoln's future. Now Lincoln was the director of the entire operation and doing an excellent job like he was born to do this type of work.

He picked up his phone and texted Lincoln.

Happy 2017.

You still up?

Need to take a drive.

Right now?

No. Tomorrow.

I'll come after the family brunch.

Perfect.

Sam plugged his phone back into the wall. He yawned. He may have just found who he had been searching for.

# CHAPTER 05

A slightly hungover, sleep-deprived, still-in-the-same-clothes-as-the-night-before twenty-six-year-old Lincoln glanced at his phone. It read 11:59 a.m. He was a little impressed that he actually made it to the annual New Year's Day family brunch early. The evening before he had made an obligatory appearance at three different parties and found them relatively dull. Nonetheless, like Sam, he had to keep up appearances that he was a rich playboy who cared only about having a good time. It was exhausting, though necessary, to divert attention off his real work with Platinum Security Group. He had hoped that his stunning date would be an excellent distraction for one single night. Unfortunately, her surface conversation practically lulled him to sleep while he was standing. His best move was to delete her contact and pray she'd never text again.

Lincoln's leg bounced to music he heard in his head. One of the songs in the club had been playing on repeat and he couldn't seem to remember the words. He glanced around the bright and artfully decorated room. His mother had it changed once a year as a sort of visual family tradition. She felt that the room should be a design representation of the up-and-coming year.

The walls were rose-colored lined with a stark-white bead

board. The table was covered in cream linen with a bed of fresh flowers running down the center of it. The china was delicately situated on the table surrounded by bronze flatware and subtly designed napkins with the letter *S* embossed on the corner to represent the family name, Silas. Even though it wasn't needed, place cards spelled out each family member's name and positioned them at the table.

One year, his mother was in a rather dark mood, and the entire room was painted black and the table was set in shades of gray. Lincoln assessed that this coming year would have an element of bliss to match his mother's current color mood.

His father, Hunter, entered the room staring at a digital report on his tablet. He was aging well, a year shy of fifty. If he had a religion aside from his devotion to work, it would have to be biohacking. Hunter believed he must optimize his body to be able to operate at its best. He was king of the strict routine. He was dressed in clean lines and his hairline was lightly wet from his post-workout shower. Unlike his father, Lincoln preferred variety and despised unending routine.

"Good morning, Father," Lincoln said.

"Ah, hello, Lincoln," Hunter said without looking up. "How were the events last night?"

"They were fine."

"What did you think of the Williamses' daughter?"

"She was nice. Not my type."

Hunter finally looked up at his son and slightly smiled, then said, "You look tired. You should have Helena put together a vitamin cocktail for you"

"I'm good."

Hunter's nutritionist, Helena, arrived and poured a cup of

coffee that included butter and some sort of oil that was specially designed for his brain. Hunter nodded his head at Helena and continued to silently read through reports. Not one to waste time, he capitalized on every second of the day.

"Good morning, Helena," Lincoln said.

"Good morning, Mr. Silas," Helena replied. "Would you like some coffee?"

"No, thank you."

Lincoln looked at his phone again for the hundredth time. His sister and mother were notoriously late to everything. He had to get out of there and meet Sam. New Year's brunch was a mandatory tradition in the Silas household, excusable only if you were hospitalized.

Twenty minutes later, his mother, Sofia, waltzed into the room clutching a Bloody Mary in her left hand. She was decked out in couture daywear that was formfitting to her tiny frame, matched her color to perfection, and complemented the decor. Her bright blue eyes shone with an uncanny delight as she approached Lincoln for a motherly embrace that included air kisses.

"Lincoln, darling, Happy New Year," she said softly.

She studied his face for a moment then reviewed his attire. "Did you forget to have your shirt pressed?"

"No, it's been pressed," said Lincoln. He left out the part that he had not changed since the evening before.

"Come, we can get a fresh shirt for you," Sofia commented.

"Mother, it's fine."

Genevieve appeared in the doorway effortlessly dressed in fast fashion with no makeup on. She grumpily landed in her chair in her perpetual state of seventeen-year-old annoyance.

"Why do we continue to do this insane tradition?" Genevieve complained.

"Go back upstairs and change, young lady. I had your outfit flown in from Paris and you will not appear wearing casual rags for our first meal together of the year as a family."

"No, thank you."

Hunter glanced up and commented, "Shall we eat?"

Sofia erupted into tears and promptly left the room.

Hunter assessed both of his children. "You know, all you have to do is show up and be impeccably dressed and all will be right with the world."

One hour later, the entire Silas family was properly dressed, with their best faces on as if nothing had transpired.

"Mother, you did wonders with this room yet again," Lincoln praised her.

Sofia lifted her Bloody Mary. "Thank you, Lincoln. I really wanted there to be a bright and airy feeling about this year. What do you think, Hunter?"

Hunter observed the room and said, "You do have a gift. Did you stay under budget?"

"You know, I did," Sofia lied.

Genevieve pushed her plate away. "The eggs are overcooked again."

"Strange, mine are perfect," Lincoln said while shoving another heaping forkful into his mouth.

"You have no discernable palate," Genevieve said.

"You're too sensitive," Lincoln replied as he looked at his phone again. He needed to leave in five minutes. He wondered how he could accomplish that, if he could concoct something to get away from the table. He clicked through his mind. He needed to manipulate this situation to his advantage.

Lincoln cleared his plate then his throat. "Mother, I've been thinking about Sam a lot today. "

Sofia nodded empathically. "I know, I invited him to brunch, but he declined because he didn't want to burden us with his sorrow."

"I wondered if it would be permissible for me to go and check on him to make sure he's okay."

"Sam doesn't need to be bothered," said Hunter.

Lincoln ignored his father. "I'd be pretty lonely without my family."

"Hunter, I must insist that Lincoln go and see him," Sofia announced.

"If you think it's best," Hunter said.

Genevieve rolled her eyes and crossed her arms.

Lincoln nodded his head as the dutiful son, kissed his mother, and headed out the door to meet Sam.

■ ■ ■

An hour later, Lincoln arrived at the Claremont Hotel and picked up Sam, who was waiting on the curb.

Lincoln pressed a button in the car, and it jammed all frequencies so that no conversations could be heard from any devices.

"We are clear to speak."

"Any update on Kaj?"

"Dr. Greystone checked him into a 'health spa.' It's a yearlong rehabilitation program."

Sam nodded. "Glad to know he's getting the help he needs."

Sam paused and looked out the window. "I think I may have found the new recruit."

"That was quick. Who is it?"

"A security guard from the Port of Oakland."

"You can't be serious, right?" Lincoln tensed up a little as he drove up the hill on Grizzly Peak Boulevard to a spot that overlooked the bay.

"There's something there," Sam wistfully said.

"Every single member of our team is remarkably talented and have résumés that elevate them to the top one percent of the nation."

"I'm aware of that."

Lincoln knew that when Sam got something in his mind, nothing could change it. No amount of manipulation or stacking the deck could make a difference, because once Sam grabbed ahold of something with a steel grip he would not let it go.

"Can I weigh in?"

"Of course. Take him through the background assessment and run him through the three phases. You can have the final say based on the results."

"Fair enough. It could be a tough sell to the team."

"I'm confident that you can convince them."

# CHAPTER 06

After a late lunch with Cooper on New Years Day, Kingston briskly walked up the sidewalk to the West Palm Retirement Home. Under normal circumstances, Papa Juan would be living with Kingston's parents instead of in some retirement home, but something had happened between Papa Juan and Kingston's dad, Tomas, a long time ago that nobody talked about. It had something to do with Tomas's twin brother, Franco, who currently lived in Costa Rica. Kingston had asked his dad about it one time and Tomas had made it clear he did not want to answer that question ever again.

Kingston's phone whistled at him. He paused and looked at his text.

Meet tomorrow at 7 a.m. Board room. Don't be late.

Kingston sighed. He knew what that meant. He shoved his phone back in his pocket.

The sliding doors pushed open at the West Palm Retirement Home and muted smells of unsavory food and cleaning chemicals greeted Kingston. He decided he would rather spend his older years in his own home surrounded by the love of his family than in a place like this. Sure, this was fine and all, but it wasn't home. He wanted the same for Papa Juan.

"Excuse me!" A nurse's voice invaded Kingston's thoughts, bringing him back into the dense recycled air. It was the lovely Nurse Alicia, who wore plastic clogs and a rumpled uniform and had a long unkempt braid that hung limply over her shoulder. Kingston was certain that she hated her job and had a case of short-term memory loss, since she couldn't seem to remember that he visited every week.

"Can I help you?" she huffed.

"Hi, Alicia, I'm here to see Juan Sebastian. I'm his grandson Kingston."

"Sign here. I think he might be in the cafeteria. That man sure does like his coffee and conversation." The call button sounded: "Code blue, room fourteen." She rolled her eyes as if to say that a patient's cardiac arrest meant she had more work to do. She waved Kingston back, dropped her overworked shoulders, then rushed off with wisps of her frizzy hair trailing behind her.

Kingston's sneakers squeaked down the hall as he passed several rooms hosting warm bodies with no life left in them. He entered the cafeteria to see a small group of men hunched around a table.

Papa Juan caught a glimpse of Kingston and exclaimed, "Here he is. 'The Hero from the Port.'" All the men cheered and clapped.

Kingston couldn't hide his delight, grinned broadly, and straightened his shoulders a bit.

"What do you think about that, Bill?" Papa Juan patted a catatonic man who sat next to him. "All right, boys. Let's pick up this discussion later. Come on, grandson. Take me around the garden." Kingston went over and wheeled Papa Juan, who was using a wheelchair as he recovered from a double knee replacement, out of the kitchen.

As soon as Kingston left the cafeteria, he deflated as he thought about how his dad would never be proud of him like Papa Juan.

Papa Juan leaned over and said hello to whomever they passed in the hallway, followed by, "This is my grandson. You might have seen him on the TV. He's a real hero."

Kingston took Papa Juan out to his favorite spot in the middle of the garden. His grandfather loved to watch the hummingbirds zip in and out all around him. Kingston parked Papa Juan's wheelchair and sunk down on the bench.

"Are you going to tell me all about your adventure or what?" Papa Juan asked in his raspy voice.

"I stopped some guys stealing from the port," Kingston replied.

"Remarkable. I'm sure all the guys at the port are jabbering about how great you are."

Kingston sighed. "More like, 'He screwed up again.' Dad's not happy with how I handled it."

"Bah! You handled it like a champ." Papa Juan bumped his elbow against Kingston's arm.

"If only I'd followed procedure and called the private security firm. I could lose my job, and I need all the money I can get."

"Oh, your dad is looking for someone to blame. Don't worry, it won't be you," said Papa Juan.

"I'm not so sure about that," said Kingston. "Jude said he was pretty mad."

"He'll calm down. He always does."

Kingston shifted forward, catching a glimpse of his grandfather's ring. It was gold, set with three chip emeralds, and inscribed on it in Spanish were the words *Love Full. Be Humble. Live Loyal. Leave a Legacy.*

Kingston asked, "Was it hard for you to leave Colombia?"

"Not a day goes by when I wish that I hadn't left my papa behind," Papa Juan replied. "But he wouldn't let me stay."

"How'd you get that ring again?"

"My papa, your great-grandpapa, was born in Boyacá, in northeastern Colombia on the border of Venezuela. During that time in Colombia, there were two different men fighting for power—a president elected by the people and a wealthy drug lord—with an emerald mine owner caught in the middle. The drug lord wanted to have the emerald mining business under his thumb to launder his money. But the mine owner could not allow it, or the government would revoke his rights in the mines. To protect himself, the mine owner had to hire a private army. The owner enlisted my papa to be the head of that army. One day, as my papa was driving the owner back to his home, they were ambushed. My papa bravely defended the owner. Everyone in the ambush died except the owner and my courageous papa.

"The owner gave my papa this emerald for saving his life. This beautiful stone was called *valiente*, which means brave one in Spanish. It had great value and was considered a gem of the finest water. I was thirteen years old at the time, and I will never forget the night that he came home with that precious gift. He was so proud.

"The Green Wars, as they were called, became more and more dangerous, and the death toll soon rose to a thousand men. My papa felt it would be best for my mama and me to travel to America and stay with his brother, who had married an American, until it was safe to come home again. So he sold the emerald, keeping just a few chips of it. He took the money and bought a passage to the United States for me and my mama. Then he found a goldsmith to create a ring. When I said goodbye to my papa, he hugged me and grabbed my hand, putting this ring on my finger. He said to me, 'Juan Sebastian, make me proud by how you live and take care of your mama.' My papa refused to leave in spite of the danger. He told me that if he were to leave, he would die on the inside, and he refused to live as a dead person, even if his loyalty cost him his life. He was killed a year later.

"King, one day this ring will be yours," said Papa Juan.

"I'm sure that Dad will give it to Jude. He's the better son," mumbled Kingston.

"Your dad won't take it. Besides, I want to give it to you," said Papa Juan affectionately.

■ ■ ■

The next morning, Kingston rolled up to the main office of the port on his motorcycle. He took off his helmet and prepared to be fired.

Before Kingston stepped into the boardroom, he felt an intense vibe rush through his body. He mentally set up a steel wall around his nerves. He took a deep breath then exhaled slowly. He felt the stress building in his chest, so his hand fiddled with his inhaler.

He observed a rectangular table at which sat the director of communications, director of security, director of human resources, port attorney, Jude and his dad. Each one had a serious look on his face.

Thankfully, his dad's face was turned away from him and directed at the flat-screen TV showing the news story of the night before with the title "Theft at Port Stopped" and footage of the thieves being hauled into the Glenn E. Dyer Detention Facility in Oakland. Then Kingston saw his face on the screen. It felt like an out-of-body experience, seeing the "Local Hero" title underneath his image on the TV. Jude caught his eye and shrugged, sending a message that there was nothing he could do to help. Kingston felt sick and braced himself for the imminent disapproval. He then heard his dad, Tomas, groan out loud as if he were in pain and pound the table with his fist. Kingston felt a wall of dread hit him hard and he stumbled into the room, making a less confident entrance than he had hoped for. Some hero he was.

The director of security motioned to the chair at the head of the table and said, "Kingston, please have a seat. Let's go ahead and recount your actions on the thirty-first of December."

Kingston's words jumbled out. "I arrived at the Port at ten p.m., and at approximately 11:35 p.m. the thieves were unloading the container."

"Let's back up. Did you hear an alarm at shipping gate C?"

"No. I wasn't in the security office."

"Why not? Where were you?"

"I was making rounds."

"You were what?"

"I had a feeling, an instinct that something felt off."

"You had a feeling?"

"Yes."

The director of security glanced at Tomas before he continued on, "Now, listen, this question is very serious, so think carefully how you answer. Kingston, were you involved with the theft?"

"No."

"Did you open the C gate for the thieves?"

"No. If I opened the gate then why would I have tried to stop them?"

"Fair enough."

Tomas eased out a sigh through his nose and interrupted the director of security. "While we appreciate the effort that you made to stop the theft. The reason we are meeting today is so that we can understand why protocol was not followed to the letter."

Kingston watched his dad struggle to be nice to him. Kingston could never live up to his high expectations. He always seemed to fail in one way or another, according to the "standards we live by as a Rais." It was exhausting to even try. Kingston knew the less he said the better.

"I think I got caught up in the moment," Kingston offered quietly.

The muscles in Tomas's jaw tightened and he said, "You do realize that the container C-10380 had over a million dollars of ANFO crystals in it? That kind of material could blow up several buildings if it got into the wrong hands. If the thieves had been successful, there's no telling how we would have recovered. Let's not forget, the insurance to cover whatever happened to the stolen goods could've been astronomical."

"I'm aware of—"

Tomas didn't listen and continued on, "Who called the press?"

"I don't know. I mean, I guess they could've been listening to the police scanner."

"Why in the world did you call the police instead of the outside security firm? What happened to protocol? Did you completely forget what you're supposed to do in an emergency?"

Kingston struggled to breathe, as if all the oxygen had been sucked out of the room. He tightly gripped his inhaler in his pocket.

I'm surprised that you were even capable of stopping the theft," needled Tomas.

Kingston shrugged. "I don't know. I guess I forgot. I mean, at least I caught 'em."

"That's supposed to make me feel better? Are you certain nothing was taken?"

Jude spoke up. "I double-checked. Inventory's good."

Tomas turned to the director of human resources and said, "What is our policy around failure to follow clearly outlined protocol?"

"Generally, the employee is written up and fined any loss of goods," the director of human resources replied.

Tomas made no eye contact with Kingston when he said, "What made you think you were qualified to speak to the press?"

"I don't know. Everything happened so fast," said Kingston.

Tomas stared hard at Kingston. "It clearly states in the employee handbook that only the director of communications is authorized to speak to the press."

"Sorry." Kingston stared at the ground.

"I think you should be suspended pending a full investigation," said Tomas.

The director of communications cleared his throat. "Sir, I agree that there should be some action in response to Mr. Rais's mistakes. But I feel that we shouldn't do that at this time. The story is actually putting the port in a positive light. Mr. Rais is trending as a hero."

Tomas caught himself before he continued with his rant. He

looked at his director of communications. "Thank you for your feedback. I will take that into consideration. "

Tomas abruptly stood up. "Okay, everybody. Let's circle up again in a few days. Kingston, please stay behind. I have a nondisclosure document you need to sign, and you are forbidden to speak to the press without our written permission."

Everyone filed out of the boardroom. Kingston sank lower in his chair. Jude gave him an apologetic look before he left the room.

Tomas paused for a second, stood up, and started pacing. "You know the problem with you? You don't think. You just act. You make things worse. It was against my better judgment to put you in that position, but Rustic's glowing recommendation gave me hope. But you, Kingston, are a disappointment. Now companies have great concerns that their cargo is in the hands of some irresponsible employee. In spite of the good publicity, this 'heroic act' makes us look really bad."

Kingston continued to avert his eyes, knowing that there was no way his dad would ever be proud of him. It made him feel tired. Tired of trying to do the impossible.

Tomas continued, "If only you could be more like your brother."

Kingston knew at that moment his best move was to listen and not say a word.

"You're lucky that the director of communications saved your job. If it were me, I would've fired you," Tomas said as he got up and left Kingston alone in the room.

# CHAPTER 07

Lincoln reclined in his chair with his eyes closed in a dimly lit control center at the Pacific One Compound. It was the West Coast home base in proximity to North America for the Platinum Security Group. It was located on an oil platform about a mile off the coast of Santa Barbara. The platform stopped producing oil in recent years, and Sam saw the opportunity to dismantle the coastal eyesore in lieu of setting up an underwater compound offshore.

The room was shaped in a half circle with stadium seating, which was all focused around the main screen. It was soundproof and required voice recognition, a numerical code, a handprint identification and a retina scan to enter.

His role from the beginning had been to strategically train and lead the team. He had personally met with several black ops divisions and they were kind enough to put him through training without being officially enlisted. His father insisted that he could participate in the field as long as he was not in harm's way. Lincoln had been able to keep that promise so far, but he couldn't guarantee that he wouldn't jump in if necessary.

The team was fresh off a challenge led by Roosevelt. It was an excursion located in the Antelope Canyon designed to be completed only by working as a team. The report seemed favorable, and they were about to meet to review the exercise.

A musical tone sounded as someone entered the room. His eyes opened to Pandora Vu. Her stark-white hair asymmetrically framed her almond eyes and narrow face. She wore black, ripped jeans with a long white graphic hoodie covered by a black bomber jacket that was speckled with white paint, a black beanie stating *Not for Sale*, and black kicks. Not big on small talk, she flicked her eyes at Lincoln.

"Hey, Pan."

"Hi," Pan said as she found her station and powered up the entire room. She set the lights to an amber setting and filled the screen with the PSG logo. She pulled a silicone cover out of her bag and fitted it to the keyboard. Then she methodically used disinfectant wipes to clean all around her station. Once finished, she placed a plastic cartoon character with dark eyes wearing a shinobi shozoku, better known as a ninja uniform, on the desk.

"Who is that?"

"As Rukia Kuchiki from the manga Bleach would say, 'My inspiration to slay the bad guys.'"

"How did the exercise go?"

"Not well."

"What happened?"

"The usual."

"I didn't see anything in the report."

"I don't know what to tell you."

"Who did the report?"

Pandora shrugged and said, "Violet." She put her wireless earbuds into her ears signaling the conversation was over.

Dr. Pharma scuttled in and pushed his glasses up his nose.

He wore blue scrubs and a white coat. "Good Morning, Mr. Silas." He took his seat up front and center.

"Dr. Pharma, how did the exercise go?"

Dr. Pharma cleared his throat and fidgeted with the pen in his hand. "The high was forty-four degrees Fahrenheit. Everyone stayed hydrated. Vitals were good. A few bumps and nicks along the route."

Roosevelt strutted in. He wore a white muscle shirt and red sport joggers rolled up to mid-calf with white tennis shoes. He sucked down a protein shake. He looked rather perturbed, not his usual positive self. Lincoln noticed a bandage on his left muscled bicep.

"How did you get that?"

"Thank Violet for that one," Roosevelt dropped into his chair.

Lucky arrived wearing a flannel shirt over a ripped rock T-shirt and jeans with a lopsided smile on his face. "I was thinkin' we might want to implement some body armor for our next exercise."

"Where's Violet?" Lincoln asked.

"Hopefully in the ocean," commented Roosevelt.

Lucky piped up, "She was right behind me."

Ten minutes later, Violet appeared. She was striking in a formfitting bodysuit. She walked in and placed herself in front of the room directly in Roosevelt's line of sight.

"Does anyone want to let me know exactly what happened on the last exercise?"

The room went uncomfortably silent.

Dr. Pharma spoke up with his tinny voice. "Violet and Roosevelt didn't agree on how to execute the exercise."

"It took everything inside of me not to knock her to next Wednesday," grumbled Roosevelt.

Violet flipped around. "Good luck with that! You would've been stuck since I helped us finish the exercise."

Roosevelt got up. "I need a minute." He then walked out of the room.

Lincoln fixed his gaze on Violet. "Is this necessary?"

"I can't handle incompetence."

It was in that moment that Lincoln realized Sam was again right on the money about the team being lopsided. He always had a good sense about what to do next. Lincoln left the room and found Roosevelt outside on the rails looking out at the moonlit sea.

"You can't let her get to you so easily."

"Sorry, it's all I can do to not rip her smart head from her body."

"You gotta tune her out. Don't let her push your buttons."

"She's good at it. She didn't do Kaj any favors either."

"What does that mean?"

"Keepin' it a hundred, she's the one responsible for Kaj being gone."

"Kaj had challenges that we were unaware of."

"She knew his weakness and she pushed him over the edge."

It was at that moment Lincoln found a crack in the foundation of their team. This fracture could either tear everything apart or be repaired so that it strengthened them. Hopefully, this new recruit would be like glue instead of a seismic event. He suddenly knew that he would have to sell the idea of a new recruit to Roosevelt. If he was on board, then he could rally in the recruit's corner.

"You know, Sam found a potential candidate for the team."

"Already?"

"I know, right? We are gonna send him through the phases and see if he sticks. If he does, I'm gonna need your support."

"Whatever you need, boss. I got your back."

Lincoln and Roosevelt re-entered the room. Lucky was playing random videos from the internet, making everyone laugh. He was good at diffusing the tension.

He had Violet, who was ground ops, great at being undercover. Lucky was good at all things mechanical. Roosevelt functioned as "the muscle", but with a surprising mental aptitude to match his athletic ability. Dr. Pharma was a master of the chemical arts and a trained physician. Pandora was the dark-web hacker, created code like a boss, and could breach her way into any security system. Kaj had excellent sniper skills and his hand-to-hand combat was off the charts.

Lincoln stepped up front and began his sales pitch. "I have an assignment for you all. I need you to vet a man named Kingston Rais."

"Wow, Kaj's bed is barely cold and we found a replacement already?" Violet asked.

Lincoln ignored her and continued on, "Roosevelt and Lucky, I'd like you to put him under surveillance. Pan, check his signature on the internet and look for anything that could be a problem, full background check. Dr. Pharma, do a health history and include his family for a full report going back five generations. I want a complete workup on him."

"You didn't assign me a role," Violet said.

"Obviously," Lincoln replied.

Sullenly, Violet went back to her seat contemplating her next move.

Pandora pulled a picture of Kingston up on the main screen. It was from his driver's license. She sorted through social media and found that he had an Instagram account but rarely posted.

His feed included a picture of Papa Juan, a container at the port, and a rubber band. He took simple, interesting shots. All black and white, and he only had nine. Pandora struggled to find a clean image of him. Then finally, she grabbed an image off his friend Cooper's page.

"His digital footprint is light," Pan commented.

"Let's get to work." Lincoln headed to the door.

Violet followed after him. "What's your problem?"

"I don't have one," Lincoln said, not slowing his pace so she had to run to catch up with him.

Violet ran to get in front of Lincoln and blocked his path. "Are you adding a new recruit into our mix?"

"Sam asked me to vet him."

Violet crossed her arms and leaned back on the railing. "Kaj was a disaster. I don't think we need anyone else."

"Noted."

Violet moaned. "Why are you being so cagey?"

"Maybe because of what you did on the last exercise. I was very clear about my directive. Roosevelt was in charge, and you usurped him then tried to cover it up. You're not a team player and now you're benched." Lincoln turned and looked her straight in the eyes.

"I can't help that I saw a better way. He refused to listen to me."

Lincoln turned around and said, "Why's that?"

"Because I'm a woman."

Lincoln laughed, shook his head, and said, "That's not the reason."

"Then what is?"

"You will have several sessions with Dr. Greystone to figure that out."

"You're being ridiculous."

"We will be stateside vetting an individual for Sam without you. We can continue this conversation upon my return after you've had a chance to consider your actions from the last exercise. Not to mention, I don't know what you did to help Kaj out the door, but don't repeat your actions, or Kaj isn't the only one we will replace."

"I can't believe you're doing this," Violet said as Lincoln turned and walked away from her.

# CHAPTER 08

According to Pan's review of Kingston's meager financials, Lincoln expected Kingston to walk through the doors of Daybreak Cafe any moment now. He sipped a café au lait out of an artfully designed ceramic bowl and pretended to scroll through his emails on his phone. His vantage point faced the door. As if on a timed schedule, Kingston Rais pushed through the door carrying his helmet at 10:10 a.m. and walked up to the counter to order. Lincoln thought he looked a little taller than he expected. The barista lit up when she saw his face. He tossed a few dollars on the counter. She pushed it back and said, "On the house."

Kingston's face turned a slight pink as he rubbed the back of his neck. He gazed down at the floor and waved her comment off as though she should be praising someone else and then made his way over to wait for his drink. Lincoln picked up his empty ceramic mug to return it to the dish bin located near Kingston. He purposefully bumped into Kingston and placed his hand on the helmet for a second.

"Hey man, sorry about that," Lincoln grinned sheepishly.

"Not a prob," Kingston said.

"Take it easy," said Lincoln as he headed out the door.

He had planted a tracker on his helmet. The tracker looked

like a simple clear, round sticker, but it was meshed with a powerful microscopic chip that sent location signals to their satellite.

Once Lincoln was outside, he said, "Pan, you got him?"

"Perfect signal."

"Send the coordinates to Lucky and Roosevelt so we can get a live tail on him," Lincoln said.

■ ■ ■

**Date: January 5**

**Location: Port of Oakland**

**Time: Midnight**

**Action: Surveillance**

**Subject: Kingston Rais**

The fog drifted down to the ground as Lincoln pulled his rental car behind a brown delivery van. The van was decked out with surveillance gear and parked near the port. Lucky had gotten a tour of the port by Kingston's brother, Jude. Posing as a potential client, he expertly placed dot-sized cameras in the security trailer, and Pandora was able to access the port's security system, so they had constant eyes on Kingston. Lincoln hopped into the van to find Roosevelt watching the feeds.

"Where's Lucky?"

"Getting a midnight snack."

"Anything interesting?"

"Not a thing," Roosevelt said as he cracked his dark-skinned knuckles out of habit.

Roosevelt and Lincoln watched Kingston as he shot rubber bands at different screens in the security trailer.

"This kid's bored," Roosevelt commented.

The van door slid open and Lucky hopped in with a brown paper bag clutched in his hand. He waved at Lincoln and then asked, "Did I miss something?"

"No," Roosevelt yawned.

"Want some?" asked Lucky as he offered up the bag stained with grease spots.

Lincoln reached in and grabbed a powdered doughnut. The plume of sugar filled the air with momentary sweetness. He took a bite and said with a mouthful, "Not bad."

Roosevelt studied the doughnuts and smelled them with his nose. He scrunched up his face and pushed the bag away. "Disgustin'. I'd prefer fresh beignets over day-old doughnuts."

Lucky stuffed one of the old doughnuts in his mouth and said, "Don't be so daft. They taste lovely."

"Aw, man, you know your palate is broke," chuckled Roosevelt.

"Who needs a palate when these are delicious." Lucky shoved another half a doughnut into his mouth, powdered sugar framing his smile.

Lincoln licked his fingers. "Don't hate on the doughnuts."

"Why aren't you answering my calls?" All three heard Rustic speak on the video feed, so they turned to the screen.

Kingston turned in his chair. "I don't know what to say."

"You can't let him get to you."

"I know. It's sick. I want his approval."

"That's something you may never get, son."

Lucky handed a doughnut across to Roosevelt. Roosevelt took it and bit into it. He scrunched up his face and said, "You have no idea what you're missing. Counterfeit pastry. Got nothing on a beignet."

**Date: January 7**

**Location: Eden Keller Apartments**

**Time: 3:55 p.m.**

**Action: Surveillance**

**Subject: Kingston Rais**

Roosevelt and Lucky were inside Kingston's one-bedroom apartment dressed as repairmen. The room was sparsely decorated, and the refrigerator was stocked with Tupperware meals marked with dates.

A three-dimensional full-body image of Lincoln materialized in Kingston's small apartment. Thanks to new technology, Lincoln was able to be present in the room even though he was actually on the other side of the city. Just by wearing virtual reality glasses, he was able to get a full picture of the room.

Lincoln was speaking, but no sound could be heard. Lucky quickly plopped down on the floor and swiped his tablet to get the sound on. "You there?"

"Can you hear me now?" Lincoln asked.

"Loud and clear," Roosevelt responded.

Lucky waved his hand through Lincoln's ghostly image. "Have you lost weight?"

"I think Pan designed my avatar ten pounds lighter," Lincoln said as he walked around the small room. "What do you got so far?"

"One very sad apartment," Roosevelt said.

Lincoln added Pan into the room. "Pandora, what have you discovered about Mr. Rais?"

Her image appeared sitting midair with no chair under her. It was as if she were floating.

"The kid's record is pretty clean. I mean, there were a few scuffles at school that were taken off his permanent record but were hidden in some notes that I had to really hunt for. It looks like his dad had something to do with cleaning up his file."

Lucky blurted out, "Oh, his dad's a piece of work. He's got something stuck up his—"

"I wasn't finished," Pandora interjected and stood up from her sitting position.

"Sorry, Pan. Let's just say the kid breathes the wrong way and he gets a lecture on the proper way to breathe."

"At least his dad is good at cleaning up messes. The only nefarious activity I could find in his family was—"

Roosevelt cut her off. "HIs momma makes tasty bites, though. My mouth was watering for those empanadas the other night."

"Your intel is that Kingston's mom cooks well?" said a very exasperated Pandora. "Could you guys let me finish?"

"Girl, don't get so mad," said Roosevelt.

Lincoln chuckled to himself when he remembered how he and Sam had found Pandora at an all-night coffee shop in Tokyo. She was completely uninterested in what they were selling until Lincoln said she could pick out her own equipment and save the world. Then she lit up and enlisted immediately. She had graduated from Stanford with a degree in computer science and was being recruited by several Silicon Valley tech companies, but she wasn't as interested in the paycheck as she was in the cause.

Pandora broke back in, "As I was saying, his uncle Franco is running some online gambling business in Costa Rica, and there have been a few questionable transactions that could be considered red flags, but from what I can tell neither Kingston nor his dad have been in contact with Franco at all. But that doesn't mean—"

"There's some beef between Papa Juan and Tomas," added Roosevelt.

"Papa Juan's my favorite," said Lucky.

"Hold up, wait a minute. Rustic's in second place?" Roosevelt asked. "You couldn't shut up about him before."

Lucky shrugged his shoulders. "It was a tough call, but Papa Juan's a saint."

"Guys, stop interrupting me, " Pandora snapped.

"Sorry," Lucky mumbled.

"Not sorry," said Roosevelt. "My intel was legit."

"The kid's growing on me, though," Lucky commented.

# CHAPTER 09

Two months after the news story broke, Kingston was still on probation at the port when his dad called him into his office before his evening shift.

Kingston dragged his feet to slow his pace. Now that the story had died down, he knew he was marching to his firing. He'd been applying like crazy to every job possible so he could have something stable to supplement his income. Rustic even mentioned that he had done some crazy reference check with a holograph of a person. But Kingston hadn't heard back from anyone.

When he approached his dad's glass-walled office, he noticed an older man dressed in a suit with no tie. His full head of loosely styled white hair almost touched his artful glasses. He looked familiar. Tomas was not in his usual seat at the helm of his desk.

Just as Kingston was about to enter the room, his dad pushed past him with Jude in tow.

"I would like to introduce my son Jude," said Tomas. "I am certain that he is the one you're really looking for, Mr. Waters."

Kingston watched this man whom his dad addressed as Mr. Waters stand and quietly look at Jude. "I'm sorry, Mr. Rais. Jude's not the one that I'm here to see."

Jude's shoulders dropped a little. Kingston had never seen his brother's posture deflate like that… ever. It was a first for him.

Mr. Waters turned and saw Kingston. He nodded his head. "Mr. Rais, this is who I'm here to see."

His dad's face showed surprise followed by the all too familiar disappointment. Jude was always his first choice and his favorite. Kingston felt like the insignificant shadow in the light from Jude's radiant sun. At least in his dad's eyes.

Mr. Waters cleared his throat, extended his hand, and said, "Hello, Kingston. My name is Sam Waters. I have a proposition for you to consider."

Kingston grasped his hand firmly and shook it. He didn't know what to say, so he nodded his head. He recognized Sam from somewhere, but he couldn't figure out where. He would've liked to take a moment to look him up.

Sam spoke to Tomas. "Mr. Rais, is there any place that I might be able to speak to Kingston privately?"

"Certainly, Mr. Waters," Tomas said lightly, then his voice tightened when he spoke to his son. "Kingston, take him to the conference room."

Kingston motioned Sam to follow him down the hall, leaving a shell-shocked Tomas and Jude behind him.

When they reached the boardroom, Kingston opened the door and allowed Sam to go in first. He quickly pulled out his phone and searched *Sam Waters*. Images popped up and he did a quick read before Sam reached his seat. Now he realized whom he was dealing with, and he wondered why in the world this billionaire was here talking to him.

Sam turned his seat toward Kingston and said, "I've heard a lot about you, Kingston."

"Me? Seriously?" Kingston couldn't hide his shock and explored his surroundings as if waiting for some camera crew to jump out and say it was all a joke.

Sam followed Kingston's gaze and laughed. "Yeah, I caught that news story and thought you might be a good fit for an internship training program that I've been working on."

Kingston responded with a note of surprise in his voice, "You want me in an internship program?"

"Yeah, I think you might be a very good fit."

"Are you sure you got the right guy?"

"I'm sure."

"Oh." Kingston scratched behind his ear. "What kind of internship is it?"

"It's a specialized team, and I think your talents are a good match. Please understand I'm unable to explain further until you pass a series of tests and sign a contract."

Kingston breathed out a long sigh and said, "Yeah, I should stop you there. I'm terrible at tests."

"It's not your typical test. I've got a feeling that you will excel at this one."

"What makes you so sure?"

"Let's just say I've got killer instincts, and they have helped me make good decisions along the way."

"I have a friend named Cooper. He's been my next-door neighbor since I was a year old. We're pretty close—that's not important. When he hears me tell the story that Sam Waters the billionaire offered me an internship, his mind will be blown. He idolizes you. He loves the stock market, venture capitalists and such. I feel like he would be a better fit, to be honest."

Sam smiled warmly at Kingston and said, "I know, I'm

asking you to try something blindly. This position that you will be applying for is related to the foundation, not the financial sector. I mean, what can it hurt to try it out? The test alone will give us both information on whether to move forward."

"No offense, Mr. Waters, but it seems too good to be true."

"I understand this seems like out of left field. But I have spent my life's work identifying talent and putting that talent in the best place possible. I believe that your talent would be a great fit for our internship."

"This is kind of hard to believe," Kingston said.

"What do you want, Kingston? I mean, what do you want out of life?"

"To get as far away as possible from here and do something that means something, I guess."

"I think you should give this a shot. It could open up a lot of other possibilities."

Kingston thought for a minute, then said, "When do I take the test?"

"As soon as you say yes," said Sam.

"That quick, huh?"

Kingston hesitated. This was his way out and he hesitated. Why was he hesitating? This was it. It was his ticket out of here.

Kingston couldn't believe the words coming out of his mouth. "Mr. Waters, I'm very interested. Is there any way I could get back to you?"

Sam smiled broadly. "Of course." Sam texted him his phone number. "Call me when you decide."

Kingston watched in disbelief as Sam got up and walked out the door. He felt hopeful that maybe this could be the something he had been waiting for.

# CHAPTER 10

Kingston woke up in the middle of the night to the sound of a downpour outside his single-paned window. Water was spilling faster than the drains could handle, sending a sheet of water down the side of his two-story apartment. He shivered and pulled the comforter tighter around him. He had talked to Papa Juan and Cooper and had decided to take a leap of faith and take the test to see if he was a good fit for the internship. The testing started in the morning. He couldn't even imagine what he was about to get himself into. He tried to go back to sleep; however, his mind was racing with what his new life could be like if he passed the test. He must've dozed off because he jumped at the sound of a phone ringing.

Kingston reached over to grab his phone, except it wasn't *his* phone that rang. He shook himself awake and started to search his room to find the phone. He found it under his bed. He answered it.

"Hello?"

"Kingston Rais?"

"Yes, this is him. How did you—"

"Better to not ask questions."

"Okay."

"I need you to follow my instructions. You need to pack—summer casual, workout clothes, and toiletries."

"Got it."

"When you hang up the phone, text all your friends and family that you will be gone on an orientation retreat with the Jefferson Waters Foundation. Tell them the location has no cell service so not to worry and that you will be in touch when you return."

"Will do."

"Lastly, upon completion of your texts, there's a thin metal box under your bed. Power off your phone and this burner phone and place them inside. Pack it with your clothes."

Kingston looked under his bed and grabbed the thin silver box.

"Found the box," Kingston said.

"A car will be by to get you in an hour. Please be waiting on the curb."

The line went dead before Kingston could get a word out of his mouth. He sat there in shock staring at the phone in his hand, wondering how they got it under his bed. He laughed out loud and got ready to go.

Five minutes before being picked up, Kingston opened his side table and grabbed two photographs. One was a photograph of a younger Papa Juan laughing, and the other one was of his mom and brother sitting side by side on the edge of a dock. He stuffed them into his bag and tossed it over his shoulder.

When he stepped outside, he saw a black sedan waiting for him. The driver hurried out of the car, grabbed Kingston's duffel bag from him, and tossed it into the trunk. Once in the car, the driver handed him another box about the size of a watch.

He opened the box and pulled out a wristband with a message attached to it that read, *Put on your right wrist.* He slid it on, and the wristband powered on automatically then pinched his skin. Kingston slightly winced.

The driver said nothing as he drove the familiar streets. Kingston looked out the window and saw years of memories staring back at him. His eyes found the lot where he and Jude had kicked around the soccer ball for hours. Then there was that tree he had climbed with Cooper, pretending they were on a mission to stop whoever was robbing all their houses. Five miles down the road, they pulled into a parking garage, parked, and the driver hopped out. A bewildered Kingston looked over his shoulder to see the driver opening the trunk. Kingston got out of the car, and the driver handed him his duffel bag and said, "I'm supposed to drop you off at this location."

Kingston stood in the middle of the empty garage and watched the car that he had just arrived in drive off. He waited there in the emptiness until minutes later an ambulance lumbered up. Kingston noticed a muscular, dark-skinned man in the driver's seat. He flashed a huge smile as he stepped out of the cab.

"Kingston, my man!" he said as he pulled Kingston into a big bear hug. "Name's Roosevelt. Ready to see if you got what it takes?"

Kingston was bewildered by the fact that this large man gave out free hugs to complete strangers. "Have we met before? At the port maybe?"

"Nah, I feel like I know you already because we watched—" Roosevelt stopped himself short and smiled. "What I'm sayin' is that we watched that news story a hundred times. Must've made me feel like I knew you." Roosevelt then swung his head in the direction of the ambulance, signaling Kingston to follow. "Come on."

Kingston noticed that Roosevelt's biceps bulged, making his paramedic's shirt appear to be almost too small. He followed after the big man, wondering how many push-ups this guy did on a regular basis. When they reached the back of the ambulance, Roosevelt swung open the doors to reveal a mobile hospital unit filled with monitors and other contraptions and a skinny, birdlike man who was studying information on the screens while taking notes.

"This is Doc. However, he likes it better when you address him as Dr. Pharma. He'll be doing your physical," said Roosevelt.

Kingston stepped up into the back of the ambulance and extended a hand, but the pale doctor looked disgusted at the thought of shaking hands.

Dr. Pharma held up his gloved hands and said, "I'd prefer to keep my hands free from all contaminates."

"Good luck, bro," said Roosevelt as he shut the doors.

Dr. Pharma pushed his Coke-bottle glasses up the bridge of his nose and said, "Mr. Rais, please take a seat."

Kingston placed his bag down at his feet and settled into the chair. He explored the ambulance with his eyes and wondered what kind of crazy job he had signed up for. He observed a monitor with a line moving up and down with the beat of a heart. He wondered whose heart was beating, and then he realized it was his.

Dr. Pharma pushed up his glasses again then spoke in a tinny voice. "Please take two deep breaths, Mr. Rais." Kingston's eyes returned back to the monitor of his beating heart and noticed that its pace had picked up.

Dr. Pharma scanned Kingston from head to toe with some sort of device. He checked the screen and read off the stats. "Height, six feet. Weight, one hundred and sixty-seven pounds. Resting heart rate, fifty-five. Your numbers look good."

"Thanks."

Dr. Pharma pressed a button that reclined the chair Kingston was sitting in until he was flat on his back. The doctor then put restraints across Kingston's arms and legs.

"Why the restraints?" asked Kingston.

Dr. Pharma's lips tightened into a thin line. "It's a safety protocol for transport."

"Where are we going?"

"That's confidential until you've gained security clearance, Mr. Rais."

Kingston nervously laughed. "What did I get myself into?"

"Nothing yet."

A screen turned on above him. Sam appeared on a live stream.

"Welcome to the Three Phases, Kingston. All your questions will be answered soon. You're about to have a three-hundred-sixty-degree experience. It will test you in many different ways. The results will let us know what type of role you might be able to play. Best of luck, Kingston, and I'll meet with you on the other side." The screen went black.

Dr. Pharma attached IV tubing to Kingston's wristband and instructed, "Okay, take another deep breath."

Kingston inhaled as a liquid traveled through the tubing and into his veins like a warm blanket. He then exhaled and his body relaxed.

Dr. Pharma reached over, checked the screen, and commented, "I'm going to push this button, and it'll put you to sleep.

When you wake up the First Phase will begin. Okay?"

"Sure, any suggestions on how to..." Kingston was asleep before he could finish his sentence.

# CHAPTER 11

Since Lucky had wired the ambulance for video and sound, Lincoln observed Kingston from the Atlantic One Compound. He heard Dr. Pharma say to Roosevelt, "Applicant B549-0 is out."

Lincoln pressed a button and switched to video chat with Roosevelt and said, "Lucky will pick you up at Mercy Medical and transport you to the airstrip."

He tracked their travel status as Lucky piloted the helicopter across the bay and landed at San Francisco International Airport, where a jet was waiting.

Ten and a half hours later, including a pit stop in Miami, the four landed in Aruba, an island off the coast of Venezuela. Lincoln had the entire dock under surveillance. He watched as Lucky and Roosevelt pushed a wooden crate to the old fishing shack near the shore. Dr. Pharma followed behind putting on a baseball cap and applying sunscreen to his hands. The shack functioned as an entrance to an underwater tram that led to the Atlantic One Compound.

The compound was a man-made island Sam had built when he first became a billionaire twenty years earlier. When Jefferson passed away, Sam transformed the island into a secured compound. It had a ground level that appeared to be an elaborate vacation home on the exterior. The interior was decked out with a laboratory, dorm rooms, a medical center, a kitchen, and an open eating space. The underwater level housed a gun range, a virtual room, a gravity room, an aquarium maze, and the central hub.

Lincoln reclined in an ergonomic chair as he waited for the team to arrive in the hub. The door automatically opened, and Pandora quietly walked to her station.

On the big screen, there was a visual outline of the entire aquarium maze. It was a difficult but short maze that was built on illusion, reflection, and automation. Lincoln had completed the maze in thirty-two minutes and forty-three seconds in spite of the fact that he knew the route going in. It was still mind-bending.

Pandora turned around in her chair. "The subject should be in place in five minutes."

Lincoln pushed himself out of his chair and relocated to the captain's seat situated in the middle of the room. "Pan, set the maze."

The submerged maze came to life as lights adjusted and the walls and floors started to move.

"Let's see what he has to offer," Lincoln said as they watched the feed of Lucky and Roosevelt position Kingston on the floor of the starting point in the maze.

Dr. Pharma got right to his station and put all Kingston's vitals up onto the screen.

Lincoln said, "Let's wake him up."

Dr. Pharma pushed a button.

# CHAPTER 12

**Date: March 6**

**Applicant Test: First Phase**

**Candidate: Kingston Rais, Applicant B549-0**

Kingston's eyes slowly opened. He was lying on a cold surface. He shook himself out of his drug-induced stupor and noticed schools of fish swimming over his head on the other side of the glass ceiling. He wondered if he was hallucinating. He lifted his body off the cold floor and saw that he was wearing a monochrome bodysuit and was in the middle of a long hallway.

He looked in both directions and made a mental note: no doors. Red lights lined where the translucent ceiling met with the white walls, creating a distinct line of symmetry. He eyed camera domes planted strategically to capture every angle. He realized he was being watched very closely. He wondered who exactly was doing the watching.

A voice came through his earpiece. "Hey, Kingston. My name is Lincoln. Your objective in the First Phase is to find the exit. Your time starts now."

Kingston studied both directions and noticed a slight reflection on the wall at the end of the hallway. It was a small visual discrepancy but big enough to send him running in the other direction.

■ ■ ■

Lucky scratched his neck and said, "Has anyone ever headed the right way? I know I didn't. I ran smack dab into the window wall."

Lincoln grinned. "I don't think I've ever heard Pan laugh so hard."

Pandora swiveled around and added, "He ran at full speed."

"Got a shiner for it," said Lucky as he winked at Pan.

"So what? The kid chose the right way. Luck of a beginner," commented Violet.

Roosevelt pumped his fist. "Actually, Vi, it's beginner's luck, and I've got a good feeling that this kid is gonna be a winner."

"It's only been thirty seconds," Violet said.

"Vitals look good. I infused the suit with his asthma medication, so he should be able to function at his best," Dr. Pharma said.

"Pandora, let's give him a push. Close the door," instructed Lincoln.

■ ■ ■

Kingston's ears caught a slight humming noise. He searched the hallway and noted a metal wall that was sliding down from the ceiling at a fast pace. Kingston sprinted and slid under the door before it completely closed.

He paused and felt winded, but his lungs weren't working against him at the moment. Kingston figured the adrenaline was keeping his asthma at bay.

The hallway configuration had radically changed compared to the one he was previously in. He stood on a small platform and studied the next stretch. He smelled something sweet. He noticed that the ceiling was opaque, and the "floor" was moving tiles floating on some sort of tracks in water. He quickly counted the movement of the tiles and realized that he would need to jump on each third space succinctly to keep moving, otherwise he would lose time waiting for a tile to return.

■ ■ ■

"Touch the water!" Lucky yelled.

"Pan, I think you were the only one who didn't touch the water," Dr. Pharma said.

"My preference is to not be wet," Pan said.

"If only I'd been patient," Violet commented.

"It was the best nap I've ever had. Never felt so rested," Lucky said.

Lincoln watched Kingston skip tiles and reviewed the time clock as he turned to face everyone in the central hub. "If he stays at this pace, he'll beat all your times."

Roosevelt was already in the midst of a victory dance, while Violet was visibly annoyed.

"If he stays at this pace, he'll surpass your record, Lincoln," Dr. Pharma noted after reviewing the stats.

They all watched in awe as Kingston weaved through the aquarium maze as though following the commands of a GPS mapping system.

■ ■ ■

Kingston reached the next hallway, which was completely translucent. See-through walls slid open and closed. He counted the movement of the walls and recognized that he could get boxed in. He investigated the hallway and saw a circular valve on the floor and noticed another one at the other end of the hall. He opened up the valve and dropped down into a tube that went parallel underneath the hallway trap. He crawled through the tight space.

■ ■ ■

In the central hub, Roosevelt stood up on his chair. "He did not just do that."

"I didn't know you could crawl underneath," Pandora said.

"No one has ever done that route," remarked Dr. Pharma.

They all watched as Kingston crawled underneath the maze and opened the valve door on the other side.

Roosevelt jumped down and smacked the table. "We got a champ!"

■ ■ ■

Back in the maze again, Kingston faced three different hallways. The one in front of him was dark, but the ones to the left and right were well lit. He knew that the glowing hallways, though comforting and obvious, would be the wrong choice. So he plunged ahead into the darkness of the hallway directly ahead, feeling the cool walls along the side.

■ ■ ■

In the central hub, Lincoln flipped around to look everyone in the eye. "Just to be clear, did anyone give him any direction?"

Pandora piped in, "No one did. All interactions are documented. Maybe this boy has mad skills."

Kingston had reached the end of the maze in record time. An alarm sounded and Pandora marked the time in the log. He had completed the maze in seven minutes and forty-seven and a half seconds.

"We got ourselves a winner," Roosevelt declared.

Violet tossed her tablet on the desk and left the room.

Lincoln waved his hand at Dr. Pharma. "Knock him out."

Dr. Pharma pressed the sedation button and Kingston crumpled to the floor.

Lucky and Roosevelt took that as their cue and headed out to move Kingston into the Second Phase.

# CHAPTER 13

**Date: March 7**

**Applicant Test: Second Phase**

**Candidate: Kingston Rais, Applicant B549-0**

Kingston woke up sitting in a chair. The room around him was stark white with an exceptionally high ceiling. He was smack dab in the middle of the room with a table in front of him and an empty chair across from him. He noticed that the chairs and the table were bolted to the ground. He thought that was odd. A few moments later, a stout, grandmotherly lady walked through a nearly invisible door. The wrinkles on her face told the story that she smiled more than frowned. Her hair was reminiscent of a dandelion puff and she wore a flower scarf, a soft beige cardigan, a pink button-down shirt, black pants, and shoes that were more comfortable than stylish.

"Hello there, Kingston. My name is Dr. Greystone," she said in a Southern drawl. "It's my responsibility to make sure that you are psychologically sound. I'm looking forward to getting to know you."

She took off her cardigan and folded it neatly on the back of the chair. Dr. Greystone eased down and opened her leather-encased tablet. "Now, why don't you tell me about yourself."

"Um, well, I'm a part-time security guard at the Port of Oakland and I deliver residential packages during the day. You probably already know that." Kingston laughed nervously then fiddled with the wristband securely fitted to his wrist. Dr. Greystone typed in notes as he continued, "If it hadn't been for a fluke news story, I don't think I'd be here."

"You don't think you deserve to be here?"

"Maybe a little."

"Your performance in the First Phase definitely showcased that you have a great deal of talent."

Kingston shifted uncomfortably in his chair. "Thanks."

■ ■ ■

Perched on the desks in the central hub, everyone except Roosevelt watched Kingston as Dr. Greystone administered her initial therapy session.

"Doc, how's his vitals?" asked Lincoln.

"Pulse elevates every time she asks a question," Dr. Pharma responded.

Roosevelt walked into the hub with a bowl of popcorn. "Did I miss anything?"

"No, Dr. Greystone is walking through basics," Pan answered.

■ ■ ■

"Did you have some sort of strategy in mind during the First Phase of testing?" Dr. Greystone asked.

"Not really. I work best in the moment," Kingston replied.

"You have excellent instincts."

Kingston half smiled, cleared his throat, and took a rubber band off his wrist. He then twirled the band around his two index fingers.

"Tell me about your family."

"Uh, my dad is an executive at the port. My mom's amazing, and my brother, Jude, is the golden boy at everything he does."

"Do you have a good relationship with each of them?"

■ ■ ■

Back in the central hub, Violet, who was encased in a formfitting bodysuit, paused before putting on her helmet for the Second Phase. "Lucky, remember when I took you out in thirty seconds?"

Lucky, who was dressed in the same skintight suit, responded while shoving a handful of popcorn in his mouth, "Correction. It was thirty-one seconds."

Violet had won the coin toss between them to be the first threat in the antigravity room. Both were very good at maneuvering and aiming at targets while in an unstable environment. Lucky was backup just in case Violet didn't take out Kingston completely.

On the screen, the therapy session continued to play out. "So, it sounds as though you don't have a really good relationship with your dad."

"More like I'm the son he doesn't give a rip about."

Violet pulled on her rubber gloves and said, "Now Dr. Greystone checks the box that says 'Daddy Issues.'"

"We've all got that box checked," Lincoln added as he swigged the last bit of his alkaline water.

"I'd love to see Dr. Greystone give Kingston's dad the

runaround. She could wreak all kinds of havoc," added Lucky.

Lincoln carefully watched Kingston and realized that he was becoming fond of the kid.

"I didn't realize that this application process was going to be so insane," came Kingston's voice from the screen.

"Yes, we find that there's an honesty in this process that really gives us a sense of who you are. My hope is that you pass all the phases so we can chat more," Dr. Greystone said calmly.

"That's our cue. Violet, you ready?" asked Lincoln.

"Can't wait to shock the kid senseless," said Violet.

"Unless he gets you first," Roosevelt rebutted. "Lucky, you'd best get yourself ready."

"Oh, don't ya worry now. I'm over-the-moon ready," said Lucky.

■ ■ ■

Back in the white room, Dr. Greystone was about to ask another question when the door slid open and then quickly shut. A female figure dressed in black appeared behind where Dr. Greystone was seated. Before Kingston could blink, the masked invader had punctured Dr. Greystone's neck with some sort of syringe and the sweet grandmother slumped over, still breathing but out cold.

Kingston defensively had already pushed himself up and behind his chair. The ceiling rushed out and was replaced with what seemed to be a thousand little spikes. The wall behind Kingston switched from a bare stark-white wall to being covered with weapons of all kinds.

Lincoln's voice came through Kingston's earpiece. "You have three objectives here. Save Dr. Greystone, don't get hit by the weapons, which are made of rubber but electric to the touch, and finally, stop your assailant."

Kingston felt his feet lift off the ground as he watched Dr. Greystone's scarf float from her neck upward, as did her unconscious body. Her cardigan hovered above her chair. Kingston wasted no time and pushed his body off his chair to Dr. Greystone's chair. He held tightly to the top of the chair with his left hand while trying to reach Dr. Greystone with his right. He grabbed her cardigan. She floated just out of reach, so he hooked his foot on the chair, and with both hands he barely grasped the fabric of her pant leg. He carefully pulled her down then guided her body underneath the table. He took the scarf from her neck and tied her arms securely to the legs of the table. He then tied the cardigan around his arm thinking it might come in handy given his gravity challenges.

During the time he was securing Dr. Greystone, the masked assailant had already made it to the weapons wall and had a spear in hand.

Kingston held on to the table leg as his body floated upward. He spotted the spear traveling directly at him. He waited a few more seconds before pushing downward onto the floor. He heard a faint hum as the weapon passed over him. When the spear hit the wall, it bent a little and a small spark arced off it.

After missing the spear, Kingston then propelled himself off the floor in the direction of the wall that unfortunately had no weapons on it. He needed solid leverage to avoid contact with any of the weapons. How was he going to get ahold of a weapon to mount any sort of counterattack? An arrow shot toward him, barely missing his head. Before the arrow could get fully past him, he grabbed the end of it. When he reached the empty wall, he pushed off with his feet and simultaneously hurled the arrow back at his assailant.

The masked invader had just flung a javelin, and the force of that action hurled her body directly in the path of the arrow. It hit her in the right shoulder. The shock instantly dropped Kingston's attacker to the floor with a *thud.*

■ ■ ■

All was quiet in the central hub until Lincoln launched out of his chair and yelled, "Lucky, get in there."

Lucky tossed aside his bowl of popcorn, shoved his helmet on his head, and took off running.

Moments later, Lucky burst through the door with a sword in hand. He sliced the weapon through the air with the intent to hit Kingston before he reached the weapons wall.

Kingston had pushed off the wall with his feet targeting the weapons wall, hoping to get on the offensive. He looked over his shoulder and caught a glimpse of the new opponent along with the sword hurdling at him.

Kingston twisted his body upside down, just missing Lucky's miscalculated thrust of his sword.

When Kingston arrived at the weapons wall, he hurled weapon after weapon in Lucky's direction.

"Better duck, Luck. This kid has got you cornered," Roosevelt yelled through Lucky's earpiece.

Lucky was still on the opposite side of the room with no weapon in his hand. He then whispered into his helmet mic. "Okay, guys, it may look like that I'm at a disadvantage, but don't be fooled. I'm about to take him down."

Lucky dodged every weapon as best he could then grabbed a hammer that barely missed his shoulder and launched it back at Kingston.

■ ■ ■

Kingston's eyes were trained on the hammer headed directly at him. He pushed off the weapons wall upward to the ceiling. Kingston felt the *zing* as the hammer just missed his left leg. He quickly wrapped Dr. Greystone's cardigan around his arm to cushion against the spikes on the ceiling. He was so thankful that Dr. Greystone had decided she needed something to keep her warm. Once he reached the ceiling, he pushed off again and sent himself downward toward the weapons wall.

Once there, he grabbed a mallet of sorts and hurled it with as much force as he could muster. The mallet was sailing at a good speed, headed for his opponent's feet. Kingston followed the mallet with a small knife that winged its way to his opponent's head.

The knife was a direct hit and its electricity pulsed through his attacker's forehead, knocking him completely out. Kingston pushed off the weapons wall and grabbed ahold of the table. Immediately, the gravity reappeared, sending Kingston crashing to the ground.

The Second Phase was complete.

■ ■ ■

Back in the central hub, Roosevelt threw popcorn everywhere, clapping and laughing out loud. "This kid knows how to win.

Nobody ever got Violet and Lucky that good."

Lincoln hid a smile and realized at that moment that Sam was completely right. He nodded to Dr. Pharma. "Knock him out."

Kingston crumpled to the ground, again.

# CHAPTER 14

**Date: March 8**

**Applicant Test: Third Phase**

**Candidate: Kingston Rais, Applicant B549-0**

When Kingston awoke, he found he was lying on something that was moving. He heard the lapping of the water against what seemed to be an inflatable raft. He wondered if he was asleep or awake. He sat up and looked around. If it weren't for the half moon, there would've been zero visibility. Lincoln's voice sounded again through the earpiece. "Think of this as an elaborate game of capture the flag, except you're the flag. Do you see that island to your left? Get to shore and make it to the warehouse at the top of the hill without getting caught."

Kingston stared at the island and calculated the most obvious places to get apprehended. He heard a slight buzz and searched all around him to see where the noise was coming from. His eyes finally adjusted, and he caught a glimpse of a small drone circling over his head. He was being watched.

He decided that the safest bet was to head toward the rocky cliffs instead of the sandy beach. He had nothing to row the raft with, so he dove into the water and swam at full speed. The water was almost warm compared to the ocean in Santa Cruz near where he grew up. He silently thanked his mom for the many years of swim team.

■ ■ ■

On top of the hill in the warehouse, Lincoln and Pandora observed Kingston from the drone feed. The tracking drone was wirelessly tethered to the band on Kingston's wrist. Anywhere the kid went the drone would follow, giving them a bird's-eye view of his every move.

"He can swim," Lincoln said.

Pandora almost laughed. "That should please Dr. Pharma."

Lincoln circled in his chair. "Remind me what happened again."

"It was the applicant before Lucky. All he knew was the dog paddle then got tired and starting flailing. Dr. P had to swim out."

"Oh, now I remember. He fought Dr. Pharma and almost made them both drown."

"I think Dr. Pharma now carries a sedative in case of rescue."

"The doctor knows how to play smart," Lincoln said.

Most of the time, applicants selected the beach as their point of entrance to the island. It's the easiest access and perfect visibility for the doctor to shoot a dart that contains his latest concoction. The Third Phase generally ended on the beach.

This morning, Dr. Pharma could not shut up about his latest serum that caused intense pain and could paralyze an assailant for ten minutes without side effects. It was like a chemical taser of sorts. Lincoln had never met anyone more passionate about his work.

"The applicant's headed to the cliff," Pandora commented.

Lincoln leaned back and exhaled. "Tell Dr. Pharma to head to the warehouse in ten minutes."

■ ■ ■

As Kingston closed in on the rocks, he began to swim under water, only coming up quietly for air. Once he reached the rock edifice, he noticed a figure sweeping the sandy beach. Even though his eyes had adjusted to the darkness, he knew that this climb would be more feeling than seeing. He reached up and grabbed the first rock that jutted out and hauled his wet body upward. By the time he reached the top, he was out of breath, and in spite of the effort his lungs continued to not give him any grief.

At the top, he faced a dense jungle. Palm trees loomed like giant shadows surrounded by smaller bushes offering the security of cover. He peeked back over the edge and saluted the unsuspecting figure on the beach then pressed through the green foliage. He stealthily moved past any natural obstacle and arrived at an open field of tall grass. He heard a crunching sound about five feet or so in front of him. He caught sight of a large figure then he heard a voice.

"Hey, Doc. You seen him?" said Roosevelt.

Kingston took three steps backward and crouched behind a watapana tree.

"I can promise you one thing. He's not getting past me," said Roosevelt.

Kingston slowly stepped backward, being careful not to make a sound. He heard the whirring of the drone above his head. He looked around and tried to find anything that he could use to create a diversion. If he cracked a branch off a bush, it would make a sound. He needed something small that he could throw far away from his location. He reached in his pocket for a rubber band and found nothing. He then realized that the drone was a dead giveaway of his location.

Kingston wrenched the wristband off his arm and tossed it in the opposite direction of where he was located. He flattened down and slowed his breathing. He heard crashing footsteps traveling away from him.

■ ■ ■

Lincoln got up out of his chair and ran his hand through his hair. "Did he take the wristband off?"

"I believe so."

"That's a first. Are you able to remotely control the drone?"

"Give me a minute." Pan hastily keyed, and code flew across her screen like a jet sweeping across the sky.

"How's it looking?"

"I got it." Pan used the arrow keys on her keyboard to circle the drone around the grassy field. The feed showed Roosevelt standing above the wristband.

"Okay, let's wait and see what happens next. Hopefully, we haven't lost him."

■ ■ ■

Kingston rapidly climbed up the tree and observed the big man below. He watched as Roosevelt reached down and picked up the wristband and looked all around him. He saw nothing but grass.

"He's got to be here somewhere. Based on where he dropped this thing, I'm headed to the tree line." Roosevelt curiously zigzagged across the field through the grass and disappeared into the trees.

Once all was quiet, Kingston looked around. He carefully watched the drone circumnavigate the edge of the grassy field flying directly in front of him. He waited until the drone followed in the direction that Roosevelt had just left. Then he slid quietly down the tree and followed Roosevelt's path through the grass. There was a reason that Roosevelt's path was so calculated. The grass covered a trap of sorts. Kingston guessed that it was some sort of pit. It was a perfect trap for an unsuspecting candidate. Kingston reached the tree cover. He noticed a clearing straight ahead. When he reached the open space, Kingston trekked around the circumference studying the tower in the middle of it. The front door would clearly have someone waiting for him, like Roosevelt, so he'd have to enter another way. He could climb to the top and enter through the open window that seemed to be some sort of lookout post. Either way, he would have to face an opponent in order to avoid capture.

Kingston studied the lookout post. He saw a silhouette of a figure at the top. He decided that scaling the building was his best bet. He counted silently, noting exactly how long it took the person to walk around the post. When the figure was on the opposite side, Kingston sprinted from cover to the building. He pressed his body against the wall and looked up. He had lucked out; the ledge of the lookout post hid him completely. He then slipped off his shoes and began his climb up the side of the building. He paused for a moment then quickened his pace when he heard a vehicle approaching on the other side of where he was climbing.

When he reached the top, he shimmied into the tower. He heard a female voice say, "Keep it down, will you? Let's not give away our location so that he has the advantage."

Seconds later, Kingston had his hand over Violet's mouth. He said, "I think I've captured the flag."

Violet pushed him backward and unhinged herself from his grip. "You're not getting past me."

She lunged toward Kingston, but he dodged her and scurried down the stairs into the warehouse. Violet ran after him, but Kingston proved too quick. He made it to the bottom of the staircase and rushed out onto the platform.

Lincoln greeted him with a loud clap of his hands. "Congratulations, Kingston. You've completed the Three Phases."

Lincoln patted Kingston on the shoulder while Dr. Pharma plunged a syringe in Kingston's neck, knocking him out cold.

# CHAPTER 15

Kingston, unconscious, was transported back to his quarters, where Dr. Pharma hooked him up to an IV of vitamins to recover. When Kingston finally woke up, he found himself curled up in a tight ball. He slowly unclenched his hands and tentatively stretched his legs. He cautiously sat up in bed, uncertain if he was about to be tested further.

His monochromatic quarters were small and sparse with a bed, a table and chair, and a dresser as furnishings. Kingston shivered and pulled the dull-colored blanket around his shoulders. He reached down and opened his bag. He pulled out the picture of Papa Juan and whispered, "Papa, I did it. At least, I think I did."

Dr. Greystone appeared at the door with a cup of something in her hand. She placed the cup on a side table next to Kingston and kindly said, "Drink this."

Kingston pushed the picture back into his bag and then hesitated as he looked at the brown liquid concoction. "What does it do?"

"I believe Dr. Pharma mentioned that it would chemically balance your system."

Kingston drank the cup of strange liquid. It was surprisingly sour, causing his mouth to pucker up, followed by a sweet aftertaste. She gently unhooked the IV and motioned for him to follow her.

Kingston trailed after Dr. Greystone down a white corridor that led to an all-white padded room. She led him to the center of the room where a circular symbol marked the floor.

"Step onto the circle and name your favorite place."

"Yosemite Falls," Kingston said.

Immediately, the room transformed into Yosemite Falls and the temperature dramatically changed to 49 degrees Fahrenheit.

Dr. Greystone softly said, "The climate in the room is real time to the location. Please consider that if you decide to go somewhere cold."

Kingston breathed deep and felt the tension in his shoulders slowly relax.

"This is the decompress room. It's important after every training and mission that you come in here and let it out."

Kingston was in a state of wonder at this experience. He hoped that he had done enough to be a part of all this.

# CHAPTER 16

Sam landed in the Dominican Republic in the late morning. He donned his straw hat and sunglasses. Many of the locals knew him well and called him Mr. Sam. He was generous and they knew it. He owned a resort near the government-protected area of Isla Saona, where he had built an additional underwater tram to the Atlantic One Compound. He felt strongly about having multiple exits from any location.

Kingston had completed all Three Phases beyond his expectations. Under normal circumstances, he would leave orientation to Lincoln. But since adding Kingston to the team was a delicate matter, he felt it best to highly encourage inclusion in person.

He entered the lobby and took the elevator down to the basement to board the tram. The tube ran under the sand for about 100 yards then it surfaced and ran along the ocean floor camouflaged by a thin screen. Lucky designed the screen in such a way that it created the illusion of the ocean floor. It took about fifteen minutes for the tram to get to the compound.

When Sam reached the water dock, Lincoln was waiting there for him.

"Good morning, Lincoln."

"Morning."

"So what do you think?"

"I'd be crazy not to add him to the team."

"Are you sure? I don't want to—"

Lincoln held up his hand and said, "He'll be a great addition once we get him integrated."

"Any way I can help?"

"One of your inspiring speeches couldn't hurt."

■ ■ ■

Lincoln and Sam entered the central hub, where the team was assembled in their usual places, as creatures of habit marking their territories in the room.

Sam stood in front of them and said, "You know, I think you've been given a bad reputation. I've heard so many negative things about your age group. But you have proved all the stories wrong with your talent and commitment to the purpose of making the world a safer place. I have to say that I've never been more invigorated about all of you as a team. You know that I was tired of giving well-trained teams that ultimately created more problems than solutions to the government. Now I feel confident that you are the solution that I have been seeking."

Sam paused and looked at all their faces. They were fully in.

"I know that the loss of Kaj is disturbing. We wish him well in his health and recovery. Maybe one day he will be in a place where he can return to be a part of another team. At least, that's my hope. Both Lincoln and I feel that we should add this new recruit into our team. All of you witnessed how well he did on the phases and we believe he will be a great asset to our team if he chooses to accept the role.

Sam looked again. Violet's expression quickly changed to irritation. Dr. Pharma showed a look of disdain. Roosevelt smiled. Lucky glanced around gauging everyone's response and nodded approval. Pan kept her reaction to herself like an excellent poker player.

Violet stood up from her chair. "I think we can manage without Kaj and this new recruit."

Sam smiled. "I don't have a doubt that you could manage through this. The intention of PSG is to eliminate harmful threats and provide a secure environment, and that must be done at a high level of precision and execution. Simply managing would not reach those expectations."

"I respectfully disagree, sir," Violet responded.

"Thank you for your feedback, Violet," Lincoln said. "But we've made the decision to move forward with Kingston."

# CHAPTER 17

Once Kingston completed the decompress session, Dr. Greystone led him out to the cafeteria. It was a large open room with a domed glass ceiling that gave a circular view as far as the eye could see in all directions. It was immediately clear to Kingston that he was in the middle of the ocean.

"This is where we eat. Our chef should be cooking up something special for you," commented Dr. Greystone.

"Where are we?" inquired Kingston.

"Mr. Waters will be here shortly to explain," said Dr. Greystone as a musical tone sounded from her phone.

"Will you excuse me? I need to address something."

A few minutes later, the chef appeared and put a plate in front of Kingston. It was his favorite dish. A full plate of huevos rancheros.

"Thanks," said Kingston as he shoved the steamy goodness as fast as he could into his mouth. The chef said nothing and disappeared before Kingston had taken a second bite.

Kingston continued to shovel the food in his mouth. He didn't realize how hungry he was until he tasted the eggs, chorizo, and avocado with a kick of spice. It reminded him of home. A woman entered the room. She was casually dressed in formfitting dark red training gear, and her hair was pulled back in a ponytail. She was effortlessly beautiful. She appeared preoccupied with her phone but then looked out the window.

"Hey," Kingston said.

The woman's head snapped up from the phone. All he saw was that she was very angry. If her eyes shot daggers, then he would be dead.

"I'm Kingston. I don't think we've met?" he said between bites.

"We have," she said.

"Oh, sorry. I think I'm still fuzzy from whatever they gave me." Kingston shoved the last bite of food into his mouth. "Man, he can cook. My mom would be impressed."

Violet coldly turned to the door and said to him, "You don't deserve to be here."

Kingston didn't know what to say as she left the room abruptly. The chef burst back in with a fresh plate of food, and it made Kingston wonder what she had against him.

# CHAPTER 18

Sam found Kingston in the cafeteria. He studied Kingston from the back. This young man had no idea how much raw talent he had. He needed training and a booster shot of confidence. Then he would be unstoppable.

Sam got into Kingston's eyeline and immediately stuck out his hand. "I don't think we have ever seen scores like these. I had a hunch that you would surprise us, but you did way more than that."

Kingston grasped Sam's hand in return and said, "Thanks. This test was definitely intense."

Sam beckoned Kingston to follow him to his office. He descended the stairs, leading Kingston to a small office with a view of the ocean. Reaching into his bag, Sam pulled out a document. "What I'm about to tell you is highly confidential, and I will need you to sign this before I can say another word."

Kingston barely read over the pages and reached for a pen.

Sam placed his hand on the document. "Kingston, this is important. Never sign without reading."

Kingston then took his time to read the document. The document read in legal terms that the candidate must keep all knowledge of Platinum Security Group confidential or he would face legal prosecution along with serious fines. Sam watched as Kingston signed the document.

Sam pushed a tablet toward Kingston. "Now, here's the more serious part. We are not a black-and-white organization. We work in the gray. That being said, since we are in the private sector, there may be times where the legality of our actions may come into question. If you get caught, then you cannot reveal we exist. Even if you do, we will deny it. Keep it quiet, and we will work to get you back. If you are good with this, then place your hand on the tablet."

Kingston could almost hear his dad's voice in his head that he was being impulsive. That he should vet the program more before making a commitment. He should be more skeptical. It was that voice that drove him crazy. It was that voice that consistently let him know how off the mark he was. For the first time, Kingston allowed that voice to fuel him in the opposite direction and to push into the unknown. If this was a big mistake, then it was his to make. This time the voice wasn't going to stop him. He put his hand on the tablet and the program scanned his handprint.

"We have a cover story prepared for you. It's what you tell everyone outside our group. You have to know it backwards and forwards. It has to be your truth. Please look at the dot on the tablet and hold real still."

Kingston held the tablet up and looked at the white dot. The tablet scanned his eye.

"Finally, Kingston do you accept this position at the Platinum Security Group?"

"Do I? Yes, a hundred percent, I accept."

Sam stood up and extended his hand. "Welcome to the team!"

"Are you serious?" said Kingston and then he followed up with a quick, "This could change everything."

"You are now a part of something that is bigger than yourself. Collectively as a group, you are meant to right wrongs before they happen. If an attack does occur, then it's your responsibility to uproot the source before another one happens. It is a cause not based on ancestry or even country. It is a cause for any and all humans."

Kingston cleared his throat. "How did this start?"

Sam stared off into the distance then said, "Twelve years ago, my son, Jefferson, decided to travel through Europe with a few of his buddies. While in London, he got on a train at 8:50 a.m. between King's Cross and Russell Square. Little did he know that a man wearing a suicide vest got on the same train as well. As a father, you go through your mind and think, was there anything that I could've done to stop this from happening? In response to this question, I decided to put together a specialized team to avert acts of terror. I want to make the world a safer place to live in. Now, I know it's foolish of me to think I can save the world. But I can work to secure it. I feel this is the only way I can honor Jefferson's death."

Kingston quietly said, "What a way to honor him."

"Thank you, Kingston." Sam waved his hand for Kingston to follow. "Come, let's get you acquainted with the Atlantic One Compound and your team."

# CHAPTER 19

Sam led him down the stairs right to the central hub. The entire team awaited his arrival. They all stood up when Sam entered followed by Kingston.

"Kingston, let me introduce you to the team," Sam said.

Kingston did a quick study of the room. There was a clean-cut, good-looking man with perfect teeth approaching him. He walked with confidence.

"I'd like to introduce you to Lincoln Silas. He's in charge of everything here, and I'd be lost without him. He makes my ideas a reality," Sam said.

Lincoln flashed a huge smile at Sam. His face was friendly. He extended his hand to Kingston.

"Kingston, well done! You have become legendary by setting the bar for every future recruit." Lincoln shook his hand firmly.

"Thanks. I tried my best," Kingston said.

"Keep showing up like that and we can definitely make the history books." Lincoln laughed then said, "That no one will ever know about except us."

Sam turned Kingston's attention to a slim girl dressed in the most stylish street clothes he'd ever seen.

"I'd like to introduce you to Pandora Vu."

She tossed two fingers up and waved then said, "To date, no one has ever completed the maze in the way that you did."

Kingston's eyes got wide. "Is that bad?"

"What she means is that you found the valve in the floor. None of us knew that was even possible," said Roosevelt.

"You met Roosevelt, right?" asked Lincoln.

Roosevelt strode up and gave Kingston a bear hug and said, "Kingston, my man, I knew when I saw you that you would represent. I had no doubt."

A lanky gentleman with tattoo sleeves on both his arms shuffled up and nodded. He had a huge goose egg in the middle of his forehead. "Call me Lucky," he said as he shook Kingston's hand.

"Okay, Lucky, were you in the no-gravity room?" asked Kingston.

"I was and you surprised me." Lucky grinned.

"Sorry about the bump," Kingston offered.

"Oh, I've had worse," Lucky replied.

Sam shifted his attention over to the angry yet beautiful lady Kingston saw earlier. "I'd like to introduce you to Violet. She was your first opponent in the zero-gravity room."

Violet flicked her eyes up at him, glared, and said, "So glad you're here."

Kingston didn't think she was that happy he was here. In fact, her body language said the opposite.

Roosevelt attacked him with another bear hug. "Bro, talk about a champ!"

Then the doctor he met in the parking garage quietly said, "Remarkable results, Mr. Rais, minus taking off your wristband."

"Pan, why don't you give Kingston a lay of the land and end

in Dr. Greystone's office for his psychiatric integration session.

"Sure," Pan said, quickly getting up and making a beeline toward the door.

# CHAPTER 20

Kingston sped up his pace to keep up with Pandora, recognizing that she was in a hurry to get somewhere and was not going to wait for him. They rushed through the main hallway, whose rounded windows gave a full view of the ocean.

"Sam built this island twenty years ago. The story, as Sam tells it, is that Jefferson had some sort of affinity for the story of Atlantis, so he built him this island as a gift."

"That's some kind of present," Kingston muttered.

"Insane, right? The entire island can fully be submerged under water so as to camouflage from above sea level."

They reached the end of the windowed hallway only to find a red hallway going downward. The floor lit up as they stepped on it.

"Remember, this place is a circle. Red to go down and blue to go up," Pan said.

"Red, down. Blue, up. Got it," Kingston said as they walked past windows that housed a medical bay and laboratory.

"You will find Dr. Pharma there regularly. In fact, Lincoln put his apartment next to the lab. Otherwise he would fall asleep at the table."

They reached a lower level with white walls and a floor that appeared to glow.

Pandora abruptly stopped in front of a gym and looked Kingston directly in the eye. Kingston noticed that she had light gray eyes and smelled like coffee mixed with jasmine.

"What's your combat poison?"

"What?"

"Like, if you could define your fighting style?"

Kingston was a little taken aback and not sure what to say. "I don't know that I've got a style. I just try to not get hit and get a punch in or two."

"Lincoln insists that we master a specific style of combat. Mine's silat. I almost ruled Roosevelt because he thought I was not practicing. I snuck into the workout room at two a.m. every day."

Pan directed him to Dr. Greystone's office. She paused outside the door and quickly warned him, "Watch your back. There's a few people on the team that will do most anything to make sure that you don't stay here."

She turned away before Kingston could say a word. He reached up and knocked on the door. He heard that cheery voice say, "Come on in, Kingston."

Kingston pushed through the door. He thought he had already passed the test, but it was just beginning.

# CHAPTER 21

In the training room, Lincoln sprinted at full speed on the treadmill. The screens around him made it appear like he was running through the forest. The smell of artificial pine filled his nostrils; even the temperature of the room matched the climate found in the dense redwood forest in Northern California. He checked his heart rate and pushed himself to go even faster. The meeting with the team did not go as well as expected.

Lincoln had recorded the meeting, so he replayed the video.

It was evident that Roosevelt and Pandora were on board. Lucky was somewhere in between, while Violet and Dr. Pharma were completely against the addition of Kingston to the team. A team split apart.

Lincoln shook his head. It was so frustrating to have felt as though they were coming in for a landing, when Kaj literally lost it with a drug-induced mental breakdown. Pan found him roaming around the aquarium maze speaking gibberish. Not sure who he was or what he was doing. Dr. Pharma did a toxicology screen and found five different prescriptions. He was lucky to be alive.

"I really think this is a waste of time. We can do this with five. I don't understand why we need to add another member," Violet argued.

Sam responded, "I hear what you are saying. We could do this with five and get by.

Dr. Pharma cleared his throat and said, "I do have significant apprehension about adding a member to the team with so little experience."

Sam paused and then continued, "What if adding one more member can give us that edge, that extra second, that advantage when lives are at stake? What if that makes the difference? I'd rather bet on extra than just getting by."

"He tested off the charts in the Three Phases. All I see is the upside," Lincoln defended.

"My instincts say that this will be problematic," Violet stated.

Sam smiled and patted her on the shoulder. "That's why I handpicked you. Honestly, you are the best at solving problems. I know that you and Dr. Pharma will find a way to make the team of six work."

Violet opened her mouth to say more but then closed it. Dr. Pharma shook his head and quietly sighed.

The main screen went blue indicating an incoming video call, and his father's assistant appeared.

"Good morning, Mr. Silas. Your father would like to speak with you. Do you have some time?" she asked.

Lincoln slowed his pace and commanded, "Stop forest run." The treadmill slowed and came to a complete stop. He stepped off, grabbed a towel, and wiped the sweat off his face. "Yep, put him on."

Lincoln's father, Hunter, appeared on screen. He was carefully situated at his desk, everything neatly placed around him. He insisted on order and became out of sorts with any sort of chaos. The custom suit he wore was freshly pressed and the shirt lightly starched. Lincoln considered suits as straitjackets and avoided them at all costs.

Lincoln took a swig of water and said, "Hello."

Hunter twisted his wedding ring around his finger. "Lincoln, I didn't see your confirmation for the family excursion."

"I plan to be there as long as there is no conflict here."

"This is a priority," said Hunter.

"I don't think I've ever heard you imply that vacation is important."

"I'm calling because your mother insists."

"Now, that makes more sense."

Hunter paused for a moment and clenched his jaw. Lincoln had seen it a million times before. It was an indication that his father was under serious pressure. He knew better than to ask because he didn't want to become the target of his father's rant.

Lincoln checked his watch then calmly said, "I've got to get going and meet with the team."

Hunter sighed and said, "Harris handed in his resignation."

"That's unexpected. He's been with the company for over ten years."

"Some company poached him. I offered to give him more money. But he refused."

"That's unfortunate."

"I can't believe that he would betray me this way. All that time I spent grooming him. Wasted."

"I'm sure that you'll find someone better." Lincoln quickly changed subjects. "Did Sam mention that we got a new recruit?"

His father looked away from the screen, distracted. "No, he didn't mention it."

"He's really green but has tremendous talent." Lincoln

continued on knowing his father wasn't truly listening, "He's all about world domination and ruling the universe. If I were to guess, I'd say we will be the best of friends."

"What was that?" asked Hunter.

"Nothing."

"Lincoln, confirm your date on the calendar."

Lincoln flipped through the calendar on his phone and accepted the invite. "Confirmed."

"Loyalty is a rare commodity." Hunter then clicked off the feed.

"What are you up to, Hunter?" Lincoln said under his breath as he tossed a water bottle up in the air and caught it.

Lincoln tossed a towel over his shoulder. He had exactly fifty-five minutes to ramp up for the cave exercise and see if he could begin to bring the team together.

# CHAPTER 22

Kingston rested on the padded examination table staring at the blank ceiling. He'd already been in the medical center with Dr. Pharma for over an hour. It was protocol for Dr. Pharma to perform a complete physical before any exercise. Kingston was both excited and nervous.

Dr. Pharma returned with a silver band in hand and said, "You are cleared for this exercise, Mr. Rais."

Kingston sat up, stretched his arms and said, "Great. I'm ready."

Dr. Pharma reached for Kingston's wrist and clamped the silver band around it.

Kingston examined the silver band while Dr. Pharma instructed, "Please do not remove this for the entirety of the exercise."

After being cleared, Kingston headed to the central hub. It bugged him a little that Violet was clearly not in favor of him joining the team. But there was nothing he could do about it except show up and prove her wrong.

When he reached the hub, he found only Pandora in the room. She appeared to be lost in thought until she noticed him. She quickly turned toward the console, pressed a few buttons, and brought up footage of Kingston in the First Phase. Kingston recognized that he was staring at a frozen image of himself. She waved Kingston over to a seat next to her. Kingston followed her lead and sat down.

Pandora fast-forwarded the video recording to the place where Kingston had removed the valve and crawled underneath the obstacle. "So, what made you choose to go that way?"

"I wanted to remove the control the maze had over me," said Kingston.

Pandora paused then leaned back and said, "Fascinating. Typically, candidates get stuck."

"Rustic always said to me. 'Lose your head. Lose your life.'"

An alert appeared on the screen and Pan said, "We need to meet at the jet. Looks like we are going to Santiago."

"As in Chile?" asked Kingston.

"Yep, we've got a nine-hour red-eye flight ahead of us."

Kingston smiled broadly and followed Pan to the underwater tram. "This is awesome."

Lincoln walked down the middle aisle during the short ride.

"Our exercise is going to be held in an abandoned mine. Your objective is to locate and secure the bomb. Here are the assignments for today's training exercise. Pan will cover tech. Dr. Pharma will oversee everyone's physical stats and therefore will not be in the field today. The rest of you will be in the field. I will run point on the mission from the hotel. The field team lead is…"

Violet almost got up as Lincoln uttered the name "Roosevelt."

Violet leaned back as if she'd been slapped and stared incredulously at Lincoln. She took a deep breath and calmly spoke. "Why? I'm on deck."

"Maybe you need more work on following?" Roosevelt challenged.

Violet flipped around. "I like to follow people who don't make mistakes."

"Hey, I make the call. You know that," Lincoln said, matching her tone coolly.

"But are you making the right call?"

Lincoln stared at Violet and responded with quiet authority, "I'm confident that I am."

The tram stopped and everyone disembarked. The tension was still thick, and no one said a word as they walked down the dock and headed over to the airfield. A private jet waited for them.

Kingston and Pan were the first to board the plane. Violet followed completely ignoring everyone.

Lincoln stepped onto the plane followed by Roosevelt, Lucky, and Dr. Pharma.

The entire team took their seats and buckled in.

Dr. Pharma went by each team member and clamped a metal bracelet on their wrists, like he did on Kingston. "I've loaded it with a great pain killer, Xanax, to relax your nerves and a caffeine kicker if you need it. Consider it equal to twelve cups of coffee. Oh, and I added a sedative for the flight." Kingston barely heard the word flight when he felt a warm rush of liquid from his right wrist and nodded off to sleep.

Hours that seemed like minutes later, the team arrived in Santiago and ended up at a high-end luxury hotel. They checked into a suite that housed a fully equipped mobile lab, control center and helipad.

Kingston observed as Lucky suited everyone, including himself, into jumpsuits that he had designed for missions such as this. The jumpsuit was made of a mesh-like fabric that was breathable and contained drinkable water. He then provided each of them with a supply bag that included flares, oxygen, food, harnesses, and belay and rappel devices.

Lucky reached into his bag again and fitted each team member with a helmet. It had night-vision interface in the visor, a real-time camera, a microphone, a screen showing a 360-degree view of the surroundings and current oxygen levels, and any information Pan chose to send them.

"Are we set, Lucky?" asked Lincoln.

"Roger that," replied Lucky.

Dr. Pharma checked each of their vitals and marked that they were good to go. Then the doctor added, "Start your oxygen at around a thousand feet. That's where the ventilation tends to get spotty."

The four boarded the helicopter, and Lucky piloted them to the entrance of the mine. Kingston's mouth was as dry as the desert, and his palms were slightly damp. He thought about how a few days ago he had been running laps around containers and now here he was on a helicopter about to go on his first training exercise, as part of an elite specialized team trained to stop terrorist attacks. He kept wondering when he was going to wake up from this dream.

Lucky suddenly sputtered out a joke to break the silence, "Violet, aren't you claustrophobic?"

"You best push your Xanax button," Roosevelt quipped.

Lucky commented under his breath, "I can tell you that it brings me great joy being under tons of rock with no fresh air."

Kingston half smiled, not sure if Lucky was joking or serious about the air. He fiddled with the rubber band on his wrist and took a deep breath. He looked over at a stoic Violet, who hadn't spoken a word or even looked at him once since they'd left the island. She had earbuds securely in her ears. She sat still as if she were stone. No emotion showed on her face.

Lincoln's face appeared on the screens in their helmet visors. "Your objective, as I stated earlier, is to retrieve the bomb, preferably without an explosion. Treat it like a real-world scenario. There will be surprises along the way that will require improvisation. Also, if you get hit with a paint pellet, it will locally numb your body where it hit you. If you're hit more than three times, you will be considered dead. Pandora, take it from here."

Pandora pulled up a map of the mine on their visors. "There should be a metal shed with four ATVs to the right of the cave. From there, head down the spiral path. You will go down about fifteen hundred feet to a platform. We don't have updated information from that point. All we know is that the device is located down there."

When the four disembarked from the helicopter and walked down the path to the entrance of the mine, they looked like astronauts traversing the moon. Lucky opened the shed and each of them motored out on an ATV to the mouth of the cave.

Roosevelt and Violet followed suit and stopped in front of the entrance waiting for Kingston. Kingston was still trying to figure out how to start the ATV when Lucky hollered, "Press the silver button."

Kingston laughed at himself and motored out. He realized that he needed to keep up or he wasn't going to prove anything.

"HQ, we are going in," stated Roosevelt as he took the lead.

Kingston then pushed the accelerator, keeping a close

distance behind Lucky, as he asked over the comm, "Anyone know what kind of mine this is?"

"It's *mina de cobre*, which means copper mine," replied Roosevelt.

"Does Sam own this mine?" asked Kingston.

"Believe that. The man hates waste, so if it's abandoned, he probably owns it. He flips them into hideouts and training locations. Not a clue how many he has."

"My guess is fifty," Lucky piped in.

HQ, we are five hundred feet down," Roosevelt reported.

Kingston wondered if his great-grandfather had ever traversed this deep as he and the others continued to follow the path down in an awkward silence, motoring past a train track with an old-school cart.

"Start your oxygen," Dr. Pharma reminded them.

Kingston reached over and pressed a button on his suit, and a breeze of oxygen swept across his face. He inhaled deeply trying to calm his nerves.

They soon reached the platform and parked their vehicles at fifteen hundred feet. They faced three different tunnels that were only accessible by foot.

"All right, King, since you got good instincts, which tunnel should we choose?" asked Roosevelt.

Kingston studied the three tunnels then clicked his microphone. "Uh, Pan, do you have any information on which tunnel we should take?"

"All I have is an old map of the tunnel on the right," Pan responded. "It stops twenty feet in, so if I were to make an educated guess, choose between the other two."

"So, it's fifty-fifty," Kingston thought out loud.

Violet couldn't contain her silence any longer. "Wouldn't it be a better idea if we split up into teams of two?"

"Violet, thank you for your opinion, but I say we stick together," said Roosevelt.

"Guys, we should split up," demanded Violet.

"What do you say, King?" asked Roosevelt.

"Left, I guess," said Kingston.

"Let's go!" Roosevelt yelled. Kingston quickly followed. Lucky looked back in Violet's direction then watched as Kingston and Roosevelt disappeared into the tunnel. Lucky took a step forward, following after the pair, and yelled, "Hey, ya loons, hold up."

Violet took a step backward, turned around, and headed into the center tunnel.

# CHAPTER 23

Back at the hotel suite, the wall was lined with screens filled with camera feeds from the mine.

"Switch to the center tunnel so I can see her," Lincoln asked.

The night-vision camera showed Violet walking down the center of the tunnel.

He tossed down his tennis ball on the floor and grabbed it back up on the return. "Apparently, Violet's not going to play nice."

"When does she ever play nice?" Pan said.

Lincoln ignored the comment and said, "Pan, I want to talk to her directly."

Pan's hands flew over the keyboard, and seconds later she said, "The line is open and only in her ears."

Violet stopped when Lincoln's voice sounded in her ear. "Violet, exactly where are you going?"

"To find the target," she said angrily.

"You know insubordination is unacceptable."

"I don't follow dumb decisions," said Violet.

"Whether you like my instruction or not, you follow it," Lincoln ordered.

"Nope, I don't. Not if it puts me at risk," Violet bit back.

Lincoln turned off his microphone and turned to Pan. "Shut down her suit."

"She won't be able to see, and the oxygen is low down there," Dr. Pharma protested.

"Keep a small amount of oxygen to keep her alive. But shut the rest down!" Lincoln yelled as he tossed his headset across the room.

Dr. Pharma clicked Violet's suit off. All three of them heard her screaming at the top of her lungs.

Dr. Pharma checked her vitals. "Her heart rate is elevated. Oxygen levels are dropping."

The camera caught Violet as she sat down. They heard her gasp for air. Then she got up slowly and shuffled back up the tunnel. Her arm brushed the wall and went numb.

She commented over the audio feed, "Really? Is this how you put me in check?"

She stumbled back out into the main area with her arm hanging limply at her side.

# CHAPTER 24

Kingston, Lucky, and Roosevelt had maneuvered through the tunnel a fair distance. When Kingston finally looked back, he saw no sign of Violet. "Where is she?"

"Oh, Violet's got a mind all her own," said Lucky.

"Should we go back and get her?" Kingston questioned as he looked back again.

"We on the clock, tick, tick. We gotta get the bomb," said Roosevelt.

Kingston clicked his comm. "Violet, are you there?" There was no answer. "Violet?" Still no answer. "Pan, do you know where Violet is?"

Back in the hotel room, Pan turned around to face Lincoln. "What do you want me to say?"

"Tell him to continue on with the exercise," said Lincoln.

Pan clicked the comm. "Continue on, please."

The farther they moved, the tighter the walls became. Lucky's butt brushed the wall and he yelped out, "Blast! The bloody wall is live." Lucky's butt went numb and was covered in a bright green color.

"Nice green butt, Luck," Roosevelt pointed out.

Lucky laughed out loud and said, "My bum is totally numb."

The three reached a dead end in the left tunnel and Roosevelt said, "Aw, man, not gonna hear the end of this. She'll never shut up about how we took the wrong tunnel. We've got thirty-seven minutes to go."

Kingston, Lucky, and Roosevelt hustled back, being extra careful not to touch the walls.

When they got back to the main platform, they found Violet lying on the ground. Lucky rushed over and picked her up. He noticed that her suit was off, and her arm was covered in green. Lucky worked to power the suit back on. Violet slowly opened her eyes and breathed out, "I'm going to kill Lincoln."

Lucky then quickly fashioned a temporary sling so that Violet could control her numbed and useless appendage. Once she was good to go, the four picked up the pace down the center tunnel, careful not to touch the walls until they reached a ledge.

Lucky investigated the drop with a flashlight and discovered an old hand-crank elevator cart that had been used to raise and lower cargo. The crank was broken, so it would have to be manually raised up and down by the main crank found on the wall.

"One of us will have to stay behind. I vote the strongest," Lucky said.

Roosevelt laughed out loud. "All right, Luck, you take the lead down there and go get us a bomb." He then made quick work raising the cart to their level.

Lucky jumped in and tested it. "Should be safe for two people."

Roosevelt said, "King, go ahead."

He lowered Kingston and Lucky at a snail's pace. When they reached the bottom, they saw a metal box sitting at the end of a narrow tunnel.

"That must be the device we're looking for," Lucky stated.

Kingston paused and said, "Can't be this easy."

"Fair point," said Lucky. He reached into the cart and picked up a small rock. He threw the rock down the tunnel, and instantly color pellets were deployed.

Kingston threw another rock and color pellets fired again. "How in the world are we going to get through this without getting hit?" he asked.

Lucky's eyes twinkled. "We're gonna be ghosts."

"Right, now how's that supposed to work?"

Lucky radioed up to Roosevelt. "Mate, would you send Vi down with the tarp from the ATVs?"

"Sure thing," responded Roosevelt. "But y'all got fifteen to wrap this up."

"All right there, Kingston, let's find us a safe spot to put the tarp."

Lucky and Kingston tossed a few more rocks and came to the conclusion that they would have to go underneath the cart elevator in order to avoid getting hit. Lucky then relayed the news to Roosevelt. "Okay, man, when you send Violet down, don't go to the bottom. We'll let you know when to stop."

Roosevelt slowly lowered Violet and stopped at Lucky's command. She dropped the tarp underneath to Lucky and Kingston. Lucky cut the tarp in half; it more than covered them from head to toe.

"Hopefully, this ghost costume will do the trick," Kingston said nervously.

"Have some faith," said Lucky as he stepped out and pellets nailed the tarp as he walked blindly down the tunnel. "And walk straight."

When the twosome reached the end of the tunnel, it opened up into a big cavern. They took off the canvas tarp and examined the box sitting smack-dab in the middle of the space. Lucky tossed out a rock and nothing happened.

They stepped forward gingerly. Nothing happened the closer they came to the box.

Lucky was about to touch the box when Kingston yelled, “Wait!” He then tossed a rock on the box and a motion-sensing gun shot a color pellet where the rock landed.

Lucky scanned the room to find where the shot of color came from. He tossed another rock and found a color launcher located on a circular track on the wall behind him. He then climbed up the rock wall and disabled the motion sensor. “All right, we should be good.”

Kingston slowed down his breathing. He cautiously touched the box, and nothing happened. He picked up the device and then a pop sounded. He looked behind him and noticed that Lucky had been shot in the leg, sending him downward.

Kingston ran to Lucky and extended a hand, but Lucky batted him away. “Get the box to Violet and come back to get me.”

Kingston raced the device to Violet and went to help Lucky. Kingston covered Lucky and helped him back to the elevator. As they were ascending, Violet grabbed ahold of Kingston’s tarp and pulled it off. Color covered his body, sending him to the ground.

“Are you off your trolley, Vi?” yelled Lucky.

“He doesn’t belong here,” she replied. “I don’t care how he did in the Three Phases. He’s not good enough for our team.”

When they reached the top, Roosevelt secured the device then picked up Violet and wiped the entire back of her body on the wall. She was incapacitated.

"You know better," said Roosevelt.

Roosevelt went back down to get Kingston. He then repeated this for Lucky.

Two hours and fifty-five minutes later, Roosevelt had delivered everything to the top, including Violet.

Back in the hotel suite, Lincoln leaned over to Pandora and said, "Push the button."

Unexpectedly, the box exploded, and color covered the team, knocking Roosevelt to the ground.

"I assume we failed," said Lucky.

"You think?" Roosevelt moaned through numb lips.

"Guess I could've done better," Kingston pushed out of his half-moving mouth.

"If you'd only listened to me," added Violet, who'd had the smarts to cover her mouth upon the detonation.

"Enough yappin', Violet," Roosevelt snarled through his teeth.

# CHAPTER 25

A month passed by quickly, and the team still wasn't united. Lincoln had been able to coach Kingston through various scenarios, and Pan, Lucky, and Roosevelt were still fully on board, but Violet and Dr. Pharma worked against the integration of Kingston to the team.

Lincoln groaned at their insane stubbornness. Reviewing the training agenda, he noticed they were scheduled for a blind exercise.

Lincoln had the warehouse reconfigured for the next training mission. Maybe the loss of one of their senses would help. Maybe a few of the obstacles would push them to work together. He shook off the feeling of hopelessness and wondered if today might be the day when they would all click and become a unit.

Lincoln personally met the team on the platform. The six physically stood together in a group, even though the chasm between them was as wide as the Grand Canyon.

"Okay, today our mission has two objectives," he said. "The first is to rescue an injured Dr. Pharma, and the second is to retrieve a canister intended to be used as a chemical weapon."

Dr. Pharma cleared his throat. "What exact injury do I have, Mr. Silas?"

"Concussion. Out cold."

"Very good. I would medicate myself; however, the last time I did so, somebody dropped me on my head." Dr. Pharma looked over the rims of his glasses at Violet.

Violet shrugged nonchalantly as if to say get over it. "It was an accident."

"Regardless, I prefer only to act as though I'm unconscious," Dr. Pharma insisted.

Lincoln opened a crate in front of them. "We're going blind on this one."

Everyone muttered complaints except Kingston, who was mystified at what that exactly meant.

"No night goggles?" asked Lucky.

Lincoln tossed black neoprene masks to each one of the team. "Completely in the dark."

Roosevelt quickly put on his mask and said, "Come on. Let's go."

"That mask suits you," Lucky complimented Roosevelt. "You should wear it all the time."

Roosevelt lifted the mask and glared at Lucky. "What you waiting for? You scared?"

Lincoln interrupted the sparring. "This listening exercise is designed to get you tuned to Pan's voice in case visibility on a mission is cut to zero. There are headphones and a microphone embedded in each mask."

"Who's the lead on this one?" asked Violet. Lincoln had been rotating through everyone as leader throughout the training, purposely skipping Kingston so as to give him a chance to build his confidence.

"Kingston, I would like you to take the lead," said Lincoln, handing him a long piece of rope. "Oh, and one more thing: you'll be tied together."

Kingston stood up and nodded confidently. He didn't react to Dr. Pharma rolling his eyes or Violet's look of complete disdain. Instead he simply took the rope and cut it in into two pieces.

"He cut the rope," observed Dr. Pharma.

Kingston handed one piece to Lucky and Roosevelt and held on to the other piece of rope while stating, "I'm assigning Roosevelt and Lucky to retrieve Dr. Pharma unharmed."

Dr. Pharma looked confused. "It's okay to cut the rope?"

"Apparently," said Lincoln.

Kingston then moved over to Violet and handed her the rope. "I'd like you with me to retrieve the canister."

Violet, annoyed, responded in kind. "I think you'd be better served if you chose someone else."

"I want you to take the lead and I'll follow," said Kingston.

A look of surprise washed over her face. "Me?"

"Yes. You have a good sense of direction."

Violet looked at him suspiciously. "Is this some sort of trick?"

Kingston raised his hands in surrender. "Not my style."

"I'll be in the central hub observing," Lincoln stated. "Dr. Pharma, come with me."

"Don't worry, Doc. I'll only bump your head lightly," Lucky remarked.

"I can still hear you. If I receive one discoloration of skin on this exercise, I promise to slip a hallucinogen into your coffee," Dr. Pharma warned.

Roosevelt pressed the mask up to the top of his forehead. "We're gonna have to put a muzzle on the doc, or he'll talk the whole time."

■ ■ ■

The big screen in the central hub was divided into quarters. Each mask had a camera embedded in the front, and Pan was getting a bird's-eye view from each person. The small screen on her tablet revealed a layout of the mission marked with each member's physical location from their wristbands, just in case the visuals failed. Her five computer screens at eye level showed the warehouse cameras with multiple views in each section to show all the action.

Lincoln entered the hub and plopped into his chair. "Let's see how this turns out."

He zoned in on the camera fixed on Kingston. He needed Kingston to decisively take the reins and give them no space to take over. He watched Kingston closely as he looked around, hesitated for a moment, and then said, "All right, guys, good luck. See you on the other side. "

Roosevelt pulled his mask over his face and Lucky stuffed his mop of hair into his headgear.

Kingston's voice came across the speakers, "Pan, you ready?"

"Ready to go," Pan replied.

"Can you call Violet and me Team Delta and call Roosevelt and Lucky Team Whiskey? Oh, and can you use separate channels for each team?"

"Done and done."

Violet and Kingston then put on their masks signaling the blind exercise was in motion.

Pandora calmly said, "Team Delta, according to our intel, the canister is located on the lower level. I'll be directing you to the elevator. This building has been abandoned and there may be some structural integrity issues, so please follow my instructions.

Okay, walk straight eight paces. You should feel a wall on your left. Put your hand on the wall. Now walk two small steps, duck down, and crawl until you feel an edge, then you should be clear to stand up. You will be at the top of a short staircase."

On the blind course, Violet quickly followed Pandora's instructions to the letter. She went at a fast pace pulling Kingston behind her. He stumbled twice. She yanked on the rope.

"Could you keep up?" Violet said sharply.

"Sorry, trying to adjust to not being able to see," he replied.

"Stop slowing me down."

"Okay."

Lincoln exhaled and crushed the plastic bottle of water next to him. "Honestly, Violet."

Pandora swapped channels and spoke to Roosevelt and Lucky. "Team Whiskey, Dr. Pharma's tracker is going off on the top floor. The west elevator is broken, so you will be going up a set of stairs."

"Oh, this is going to be grand," heralded Lucky.

"Maybe if you showed up to a workout, might not be so hard," jabbed Roosevelt.

Pan cut in, "Team Whiskey, count ten steps and turn right then count another ten. Repeat six times."

Pan changed the channel back to Violet and Kingston. "Take five steps down and follow to the end of the hallway." When Kingston and Violet reached the end of the hall, a siren started blaring so loud that it drowned out Pandora's voice on the comms.

Violet tapped her ears and said, "Pan, turn on the acoustic filters and tune the frequency to the tone of your voice."

Pan turned on the frequency and the alarm sound in Violet's and Kingston's ears disappeared.

“Good call, Violet,” Kingston complimented.

Pandora continued with instructions, “Move to your right and follow the wall. Don’t drift forward or you will fall twenty feet.”

Pan switched back over to Roosevelt and Lucky. “Guys, is everything okay? You are stuck on the fifth flight of stairs.”

Roosevelt chuckled. Lucky was bent over trying to catch his breath, held up his hand, and said in between gasps for oxygen, “I’m a tad winded.”

Roosevelt railed Lucky, “The good doc could die ’cause of your laziness.”

Lucky tried to push himself up. “Just.” He leaned against the wall. “Give.” Then slid down the wall. “Me.” And finally said breathlessly, “A moment.”

Roosevelt, annoyed, tossed Lucky over his shoulder and headed up the next flight of stairs. “No way we gonna fail ’cause you can’t keep up.”

Lucky struggled for a second and then gave up. Pan pinged back over to Violet and Kingston as the hallway started to shake. Violet lost her balance, fell forward, and hit the ground. The rope tugged Kingston hard, almost causing him to lose his footing.

Kingston reached out in the darkness and his foot bumped up against the bottom of Violet’s foot. “Don’t step on me,” she demanded.

Kingston stopped and took a step back. “You okay?”

Violet got back onto her feet and muttered, “I’m fine.”

Lincoln sighed with frustration. “Block in Team Delta. Maybe this will force a conversation.”

“Okay, you both are coming up to an elevator. I’m opening the doors. Go ahead and step in. I’ll take you down to the subterranean level,” Pan instructed.

# CHAPTER 26

Violet and Kingston stepped onto the elevator and felt around the walls to find a place to stand. The elevator went down a few floors then came to a stop and the doors opened. Violet warily stepped out with Kingston tethered behind her. Pandora's voice started going in and out. "Team—" Then static. "Go right—" More static. "Down—" Then full static.

Violet shifted her pace to the right and then ran straight into the wall. Kingston bumped into her. Then a slight vibration happened. Violet turned back around and headed back the other way to only find another wall.

Violet became very still. "Please no."

All Kingston heard was static. "Pan, any instructions?"

Violet ripped off her mask and began to hyperventilate. They were walled in completely in a five-foot by ten-foot space illuminated only by pinholes of light. She searched all over for some way out and realized that they were stuck in the small area. She slammed the walls with her fists frantically trying to find a way out. Her breath quickened and her heart pounded in her ears as a cold sweat covered her body.

She desperately flipped around and said in between jagged breaths, "Take your mask off."

"If we take our masks off, do we fail the mission?" Kingston asked.

"We got caught in a trap. We have to figure our way out."

Kingston yanked off his mask and pulled out his flashlight to check for any exit points. Violet stumbled then blacked out and fell backward. Kingston caught her before she hit the ground.

Kingston checked his phone, but it said NO SERVICE. He couldn't get any help from Lincoln on this one. He had to navigate this on his own.

Violet's body jolted to consciousness. Her head was lying in Kingston's lap. She pushed herself up and immediately got woozy again. She steadied herself and crawled to the opposite wall.

"Was this your brilliant idea? Get me in a small space, trap me, and force a relationship? Are you in cahoots with Lincoln?"

Kingston didn't bother to answer and absentmindedly reached into his pocket to pull out his rubber band. He then stretched the rubber band between two thumbs and began twirling it slowly.

Silence encased them, and finally Violet spoke out of desperation so as to not think about the walls closing in around her. "Why do you always play with that rubber band?"

Kingston shrugged it off and quickly put the rubber band back into his pocket. "I don't know. I mean, I guess it helps me focus."

The silence arrived again.

Kingston stood up and stretched then sat back down. He finally couldn't take it anymore and pulled out the rubber band again.

"Seriously, what's with the rubber band?" Violet grumbled.

Kingston sighed. "I don't know. It reminds me of home.

It reminds me where I came from. I guess I always thought of myself as a rubber band, stretching to reach everyone around me one way or another. It's random, I know."

Violet didn't say one word, so Kingston continued on.

"My brother and I would spend hours running around at the Port of Oakland. One day, when my parents were out of town, Papa Juan showed up with a bag of marbles to play with while he was working a shift. We found some rubber bands in the office and the marble war began. Jude and I chased each other around the containers. It was super fun until I nailed my brother in the mouth and knocked out his front tooth."

"Bet your brother loved that."

"Oh, he got over it. He begged my dad for a gold tooth as a replacement. He wanted to be a modern-day hustler."

The silence returned.

Back in the enclosed space, one hour had passed. Kingston and Violet continued to sit in silence until finally Violet spoke. "I was an only child growing up, and I always wondered what it would be like to have a sibling."

"Yeah, it's okay, I guess," Kingston replied. "At least as an only child you get your parents' full attention. Nobody chooses a favorite."

"Let me guess, you're not the favorite?"

He shrugged his shoulders and quickly changed the subject. "One time, my brother and I were playing hide-and-seek at the port. I had this brilliant idea to hide in one of the shipping containers. Little did I know that the container was set to ship to China the next day. When I couldn't be found, my dad tore open every container and found me asleep on top of a bunch of bottled water."

"It would have been freaky to wake up in China," said Violet.

"For real."

Kingston and Violet sat in silence for a few more minutes. "It sounds like you have a good dad," she said.

"Nope. It's the only time I thought he really cared about me."

Violet danced the beam of her flashlight in between the pinholes of light across the dark space of the wall. "My parents were incredibly protective of me. Sometimes I wonder how everything would've turned out if they hadn't…" Her voice trailed off.

Kingston didn't say a word. He leaned over and squeezed her arm. Violet pulled away from him. "I don't want to be in here all day. Where is the rest of our team?"

"Maybe they got stuck as well?"

# CHAPTER 27

Back in central hub, Pandora twirled around in her chair and commented, "At least she's being civil."

"A hint of progress," Lincoln responded. "Let's give them a bit more time."

Upstairs, Team Whiskey had reached Dr. Pharma and was clumsily strapping him to a stretcher when Pandora pressed a button to change the configuration of the stairs for Lucky and Roosevelt's return. Lincoln watched the screens as the stairs moved, revealing gaps.

Pandora clicked a button. "Team Whiskey, I have to take you down a different set of stairs. The other ones are blocked."

On screen, Roosevelt and Lucky hauled a securely strapped Dr. Pharma on the stretcher to the new set of stairs. They were blindly approaching a gap.

"Team Whiskey, you will need to remove your masks for this part of the staircase," Pan said. "There is a four-foot gap that you will need to cross."

Both of the guys pulled off their masks, put them in their pockets, and looked downward. Lucky whistled low and smooth.

"What's the matter?" said Dr. Pharma as he tried to sit up.

Lucky reached into his pocket, took out his mask, and used it to cover Dr. Pharma's head.

"Don't cover my face," said a muffled Dr. Pharma.

Then Lucky took a medicated strip from his other pocket and put it on Dr. Pharma's wrist. The strip dissolved into the doctor's skin and caused him to fall asleep instantly.

Lucky shrugged. "Now I can hear myself think."

"Best thing you've done all day," said Roosevelt.

Roosevelt and Lucky reached the place where they had started on the main floor with Dr. Pharma and now stood there wondering where Violet and Kingston were. Roosevelt was certain he and Lucky would be last to arrive.

"Hey, Pan," said Lucky, "where's Team Delta?"

"We're in a holding pattern per Lincoln," Pandora responded. "Wait for further instructions."

Lincoln watched the clock. Both Kingston and Violet remained silent for another two hours. Lincoln took off his headset and tossed it down on the console. "I've had enough. Get them out of there."

Pan pressed a button and spoke clearly. "Team Whiskey, we need you to retrieve Team Delta. They are trapped in a lockdown room on the level below you. You will need to manually pull the lever adjacent to the room."

Roosevelt and Lucky put their blindfolds back on and followed Pan's voice down to the lockdown room. It took the pair of them another half hour to find and pull the lever.

Violet looked up at both of them and said, "What took you so long?"

"We got held up," Lucky said.

"Sure you did," whipped back Violet.

# CHAPTER 28

Sitting in a restaurant, Hunter checked his one-of-a-kind watch made by the hand of an incredibly skilled watchmaker and noted that Sam was already eleven minutes late. Ever since the death of his wife, Sam seemed to arrive later and later with no concern for whomever was waiting. He was on his own clock. Hunter wondered if he should suggest more therapy with Dr. Greystone. It seemed to have worked wonders with Sofia, Genevieve, and Lincoln, but Sam was old-school and probably would be insulted at the suggestion. Thankfully, Hunter had scheduled their tee time forty-five minutes later so that this "grief" tardiness wouldn't hinder their game.

Hunter would never forget the day when he met Sam Waters. It had been during his last year at Harvard and he had been assigned to host the multimillionaire for a business workshop. He and Sam hit it off right away, and Sam hired Hunter straight out of college. At the time, Titanium Fortress Investments was a simple money management firm that exclusively managed the high-net-worth assets of wealthy individuals that Sam had personal relationships with. But Hunter had the foresight to acquire a few companies that transformed TFI into what it is today: a billion-dollar company.

Sam was like a second father to him. Hunter couldn't believe that it had been three years since they'd sat in this exact place and Sam tossed him the keys to his office. Sam had glanced at him, fighting tears from his eyes, and said, "It's time for you to sit in the driver's seat." Sam had decided to step down when his wife was diagnosed with stage four ovarian cancer.

Hunter heard an unfamiliar voice. "Hunter Silas, is that you?"

Hunter turned toward the voice and looked at a distant familiar face. The gentleman was dressed casually in a blue-striped collared shirt, white pants, and a white ball cap. He had beady dark eyes and pale skin.

Hunter put on a smile and nodded his head. "Yes, it is. How long has it been?" he asked, hoping that the question would give him more clues as to who was speaking to him.

"Let's see, I mean, I don't think we've seen each other since college."

It hit Hunter that he was speaking to Alexis Harlford. He realized he didn't recognize him because he used to only wear hoodies and jeans.

"Alexis, good to see you."

"I've reached out to your assistant a few times and never heard back."

"Oh really? I'll have to talk to her about that."

"We should get together and catch up sometime. I think your company might be interested in something that I'm doing."

Alexis handed Hunter his business card.

"Yes, I will get in touch with you."

Five minutes later, Sam arrived with a proud look on his face. "Hunter! Have you been waiting long?" Sam didn't wait for an answer as he gave Hunter a huge hug and wasted no time asking, “How are you doing?”

“I’m well,” Hunter replied as he signaled the waiter. “I had them whip up your favorite, grilled cheese and tomato soup with a glass of water, no ice.”

“Thanks, I’m famished. How’s Sofia?”

“Sofia’s good. She’s wrapped up in the host committee for the Future Trust Gala. By the way, do you plan to attend this year?”

Sam lightly wiped the corners of his mouth and smiled. “I suppose I should. I don’t like small talk much, though.”

“It would mean the world to Sofia. I think the Crown Prince may attend this year.”

“Funny how a small gathering has turned into such an event. How’s Genevieve?”

“Oh, Genevieve excels at everything she does. Right now, she has an impressive GPA of four point eight, and it’s only her junior year. Several universities want to give her a full-ride scholarship.”

Sam stirred his soup slowly then said, “She takes after her father.”

Hunter was about to reply when a waiter announced it was their tee time at the clubhouse.

Sam stirred his soup slowly, making no movement to leave. “I looked at your quarterly reporting, and the company looks healthy. How are you doing?”

Hunter smiled. “I’m fine. But you know there’s always room to expand.”

Sam sat back resolutely and pushed his half-eaten soup away from him. “True. You are gifted at that for sure. Never was my thing.”

"Should we head out?" asked Hunter.

"Yeah, let's get this game started. I gotta knock the rust out." Sam folded his napkin precisely, stood up, and placed the napkin on his chair.

When they arrived at the course, Hunter wasted no time. He set his ball on the tee and whacked it. The ball sailed high in the air and landed nowhere near the green. A spark of anger washed over Hunter's expression, but he cleared it, turned in the direction of Sam, and said, "As many lessons I've taken, I never seem to improve at this game."

He chuckled. "Maybe you need to relax a little?"

Sam ambled up and swung his club with ease. The ball sailed through the air. A perfect shot that landed on the green. He then motioned to the caddy to bring up the bags, sensing that Hunter did not want to be overheard. The caddy expertly placed the two bags next to them.

"Thank you, son. We will be hauling our own bags in the cart today," Sam said as he slid cash into the caddy's hand.

"Sure thing, Mr. Waters, and thank you," said the caddy as he walked away from the two men.

Sam and Hunter got into the cart and made their way over to the green.

"What can I help you with, Hunter?" Sam asked.

"I've been thinking. You know, my ultimate goal has been to groom Lincoln to take over the company one day. I think the time has come for him to transition over to TFI.

"Oh really?"

"A spot opened up in the marketing department, and I believe it would be a good fit for him."

Sam whistled. "I knew this day was coming. Thought I

had a little more time, but I always seem to think that time is unlimited."

"It would be the natural next step now that Lincoln's got a great deal of experience leading under his belt."

Sam didn't utter a word as he surveyed the scope of the golf course. Hunter shifted his weight back and forth, not sure what to say.

Finally, Sam said, "Makes perfect sense. He's definitely got what it takes."

Hunter let out a big sigh. "I was concerned that you'd be opposed to it."

"Of course not!" Sam's eyes twinkled. "Is he excited about it?"

"I haven't talked to him about it officially. I wanted to get your blessing first."

"You have it. We will miss him, though. He's really built the training program from scratch."

"Have you secured any new government contracts for this specialized group?"

"You know, after giving it considerable thought, I'd rather work around them."

"I didn't know that you were such an outlaw."

"There is government, and there is smart. If smart makes me an outlaw, then so be it."

"You continue to surprise me, Sam," said Hunter as he stepped up to the ball. He stiffly swung and managed an okay shot up and out.

The two walked over to where the ball had landed and Sam said, "By the way, we got this new recruit. I think he's going to be one of our best yet. Once we get the edges smoothed out."

"Lincoln mentioned him," said Hunter as he hit the ball again and it came to the edge of the green near Sam's ball. Sam leaned on his putter as Hunter stepped up to his ball. Then after several attempts Hunter sunk the ball into the hole.

"There you go, Hunter."

Sam and Hunter continued on with the game. As per usual, Sam's consistent, relaxed swing ushered the ball easily onto the green, while Hunter grew more agitated with each missed shot.

Sam held back a chuckle as Hunter tossed his golf club across the course and suggested, "Maybe we should take up a new active meeting?"

Hunter winced to control his rage. "No. It's fine. I can handle it. Just need to take a moment." Hunter stretched his arms up and breathed deeply then said, "Be the ball."

Sam effortlessly swung his club with perfect form and the ball sailed through the air, landing on the green, which caused Hunter to curse beneath his breath.

"Sorry, you were saying something about the new recruit?" he then asked.

Sam smirked. "On paper, he might not look like the right choice, but I've got a good feeling about this kid. Kinda the same feeling I had when I met you."

Hunter's eyes couldn't hide the aggravation with the game when he said, "Hopefully, he's worth a million-dollar investment."

"I think he is. Besides, it almost seems serendipitous with Lincoln's transition," commented Sam.

Hunter leaned back and surmised, "He certainly has big shoes to fill."

"Yes, he does," said Sam. "Could I ask a favor of you?"

"Name it, Sam."

"Could you give me a nine-month transition period?"
"I can work with that."
As always they shook hands to show the deal was done.

# CHAPTER 29

Sam knew Hunter wouldn't be patient for long. The team had experienced so much change with the addition of Kingston. It had only been ninety days since they had added him to the team. They had been on six training exercises, multiple group therapy sessions, and a strict daily regimen in between. The regimen worked on hand-to-hand combat, target practice, team building, threat anticipation, and problem resolution challenges. Eat. Sleep. Repeat. The scores were high for everyone except for the team-building portion. They were a team divided and winning at being separate. He needed to strategize a way to bring them together and find a smart way to transition the team to functioning independently without Lincoln.

Sam knew that he had to get in the mix. He immediately boarded his plane and flew down to the Dominican Republic. He scheduled a morning meeting with Lincoln and Dr. Greystone to review the progress of the team.

Sam and Lincoln observed onscreen the activity in the white room as the team was being hooked up to the emotional management system. It was an elaborate patch and wireless system that monitored responses, like heart rate and temperature, to give authentic emotional indicators.

"Where we at, Lincoln?"

"Our up is down and our left is right."

Sam scanned Pandora's stats, knowing they would remain constant as long as she was her cool and distant self. Violet's stats spiked up and down as she picked at the edges of her nails while still managing to look stunning. Roosevelt's stats were on tilt as he paced like a caged animal because he would rather be in the gym working out his aggression than stuck in a room discussing his feelings. Dr. Pharma's numbers barely registered, as he was preoccupied, as usual, with typing notes on his smart phone. Lucky stayed his good-humored self, cracking jokes and laughing at them as he tried to amuse Pandora. Sam's eyes settled on Kingston. He seemed quiet, but his numbers were telling a different story. His heart rate was racing, and his temperature was a bit elevated.

"What about Kingston?"

"It's so frustrating because for every inch of progress he makes, he gets sent two steps backward."

"Do you think we should remove Violet from the equation?"

Lincoln looked surprised then said, "No, she's as much a benefit as she is a liability. "

"Okay, let's make this work."

Dr. Greystone entered the hub. She smelled baby-powder fresh. In her warm, genuine voice, she asked, "Sam, how are you?

"Well enough. I'd be better if this team would get in sync so we can get out in the field," said Sam.

"It's only been three months. There really hasn't been an opportunity to develop enough trust to defeat the competition, not to mention the jealousy."

"How long do you think it will take them to get there?"

"Not sure. I should get to work. Feel free to watch the session on the screens," Dr. Greystone said as she patted his arm.

**Date: June 9**

**Exercise: Group Therapy Session with Dr. Greystone**

**Attendance: Kingston Rais, Dr. Ray Pharma, Lucky Richmond, Pandora Vu, Violet Baudouin, and Roosevelt Walker**

The entire team sat in a half circle in the white room. Dr. Greystone said nothing and examined each of them while reviewing current readouts on her handheld tablet.

"First of all, I would like to thank you all for attending our session today," Dr. Greystone said.

"As if we had a choice," Lucky said sarcastically.

"That may be, but your performance on the last six exercises, while some have been completed, has been extremely poor in the area of teamwork and not up to the standard at which you need to be functioning. It's imperative that your emotional issues don't hinder the team during missions."

Violet kept fidgeting in her chair, so Dr. Greystone pushed a button that activated restraints around her waist, wrists, and ankles.

Violet rolled her eyes. "Is this really necessary?"

"Consider it assistance to calm your nerves, because it's affecting my readings. But you already know that, my dear," said Dr. Greystone.

"You know what I know? That he shouldn't be a part of this team," Violet snapped.

"I think that's a gross generalization, Violet, and given your experience, you should be helping him assimilate into the team."

"Here, here," Lucky said.

Dr. Greystone clicked her tongue at Lucky. "Lucky, don't be so quick to judge. I've reviewed the tapes, and you've been compliant; however, I haven't seen you go the extra mile."

"Fair enough," admitted Lucky.

"Kingston, would you mind sharing with the group how you felt about the most recent exercise?"

Kingston cleared his throat. "At first, I felt excited about working on our speed. Then I ran into a wall."

"Named Violet," Roosevelt said.

Dr. Greystone sharply looked at Roosevelt.

Kingston nervously fidgeted with the rubber band around his wrist. "I was able to complete the exercise in spite of not being able to breathe."

"He turned blue. It was awful," said Lucky.

"We woulda had a shot if Violet hadn't given him the wrong wristband and he had the asthma juice," jabbed Roosevelt.

"I had no idea that it was the wrong wristband," Violet commented sharply back.

"Kingston, do not accept any wristband from anyone except me," Dr. Pharma instructed.

Dr. Greystone looked sharply at the four outspoken offenders and pressed a button on her tablet. It sent all four chairs in a backward sliding motion, knocking the wind out of each one of them.

"Apparently, you've forgotten the rules here. It's not your time to talk. I was speaking to Kingston." She then looked at Kingston. "Please continue to elaborate. What could've made the mission more successful?"

Kingston sighed, "I don't know. All I know is that I'm not

the enemy. But some members think I am. All I've ever wanted to do is make some sort of difference—to leave the world a better place. I think that I can do that here. I want to do that here."

Violet cut off Kingston. "Sure you do—"

Before Violet could get out another word, she was pulled up out of her chair and hung upside down by one ankle. It startled Kingston to see Violet slowly spinning in the air.

"Just accept the boy, Vi, so we can move on," Lucky said.

Dr. Greystone pressed the button, and Lucky was hanging alongside Violet.

"Admission is the first step to change, Kingston. Group unification is never an easy process, but I feel like we need to focus and talk through our conflict first, so we can find a place of resolution. Now, Violet, you seemed threatened by Kingston?"

"Ha! He's not remotely any type of threat!" Violet said as she spun slowly.

"Why are you acting like it then?"

"I'm not—" Violet then bit her lip.

Dr. Greystone lowered Violet back down to the floor.

"What exactly did Kingston do to you personally to merit such a response?"

"He should've been here from the start. He's not a good enough replacement for Kaj. He's inexperienced. Slightly talented."

"So you want him to pay some sort of dues? In order to justify his place."

"Potentially true."

"Let's follow that thought. Did you create this program?"

"No."

"Okay, did you establish the guidelines and rules?"

"No."

"Then why are you attributing self-made rules to how Lincoln operates the team?"

Violet sat silently.

"How about this? Why are you taking your anger out on someone who is not actually in charge of the program?"

Sam leaned back in his chair and muted the sound of the session. "I've been thinking that I'd like to come back and get more involved here."

Lincoln's face contorted with confusion for a brief second then returned to a relaxed demeanor. "Everything okay?"

"Yes, I'm finally in a better headspace, and I want to be useful again."

"Will we go back to the original structure?"

"No, son. Let's collaborate and get this team up and running."

Sam glanced over and caught Lincoln letting out a sigh. At that moment, he realized that Lincoln's transition would not be easy at all.

# CHAPTER 30

Kingston woke up with a start. Something felt off. He looked around the room and searched for something, not sure what it was he was looking for. Nothing seemed out of place. Then it hit him: a few moments ago, Papa Juan was sitting on the edge of his bed. It was eerily real, even though it was a dream. Papa Juan kept trying to speak to him in some strange language. Kingston had tried to tell him over and over again that he didn't understand what he was saying, and Papa Juan had flailed his arms in frustration that he couldn't get his message across. Kingston had only seen Papa Juan do that once before, when he was trying to make things right with his dad and Tomas had refused to listen. Normally, his dreams were undertones, not so vivid. More like whispers, shapes, and abstracts. This dream was so true-to-life that he could see the wrinkle lines around Papa Juan's eyes. Kingston wondered if it was some sort of sign to call home, but outgoing phone calls were usually reserved for the weekends. Though he wondered if Lincoln would make an exception for this dream. Yeah, that conversation would probably not go so well. He would only sound legitimately insane, and the last thing he needed was something else to mark his uneasy standing with the team. Kingston pushed the dream from his mind and chalked it up to stress.

■ ■ ■

At breakfast, Kingston numbly observed the divide between the team. On one side of the room, Violet and Dr. Pharma quietly ate while scrolling through their tablets. Lucky and Roosevelt were laughing about something. Pandora was carrying a tray of food in the direction of the central hub. Before he had a chance to pull up a chair at Lucky and Roosevelt's table, a hand pressed on Kingston's shoulder and he turned around to see Sam. Kingston thought that he looked almost sad. Sam nodded toward the door and Kingston followed him.

Sam led Kingston up to his office, to the same place where all his training had begun. It seemed like ages ago, when in reality it had only been a matter of months. Sam appeared nervous. Kingston had never seen him so uneasy. He usually was very even-keeled. Sam cleared his throat and looked around, trying to find the right words. "Son, I received a message from your mother…your grandfather passed away last night."

Kingston felt as though he had been slammed into a wall, making him step backward almost to the point of losing his footing. He steadied himself then turned away quickly and tried to forcefully push down the sobs. He remembered Papa Juan looking so strong before he'd left. Had he known his goodbye was final, he might've stayed longer. He might've never left. All the energy drained out of him as he looked out at a tranquil sea. He realized at that moment that he would never be able to talk with his hero again. Out of sheer respect, Kingston allowed a few silent tears to drip off his face.

Sam lightly squeezed Kingston's shoulder. "In my experience, closure is very important. It's hard to move forward without it. Why don't you head on home for the funeral and say your goodbyes?"

Kingston wiped his eyes and barely got out the words "He's really gone?"

Sam responded with a break in his voice, "Yes, he is."

■ ■ ■

Three days later, Kingston ambled into the chapel in a daze. He shoved all his emotions into a dark closet so that his dad wouldn't be humiliated by his weakness. He admired the many gray heads in the room. Papa Juan had been well respected by many longshoremen, port executives, and union members. He was always so good with people and knew how to bring out the best in them. Kingston recognized many faces that lived in his childhood memories. He looked over and saw his uncle Franco. It had been about ten years since Kingston had seen him last. Franco fidgeted uncomfortably with his white starched shirt, which almost glowed in contrast to his uncle's Costa Rican sun-bronzed skin. His dark, unruly curls were carefully slicked back. Funerals always brought together all kinds of estranged relatives.

Kingston caught Jude out of the corner of his eye. He didn't have energy to speak, so he walked straight past him and toward Papa Juan's lifeless body. He heard the echo of his hearty laugh in his head.

Everything inside of Kingston wished that his grandfather would sit up and have just one more conversation. Yet, Papa Juan was perfectly still and appeared smaller than Kingston remembered. His shoulders were caved in. The same strong shoulders that used to carry him around the port. He looked down at his grandfather's perfectly folded hands and noticed the tan line from his ring. Kingston wondered who had the ring.

Papa Juan was truly gone. Kingston quickly walked away and sat down as soon as the tears threatened to exit his eyes.

Kingston heard Jude's voice. "Bro, it's been a while. You okay?"

Kingston nodded his head but didn't say a word. Jude reached around and rested his arm on his brother's shoulders. "Papa Juan's free now. He has no pain and is making new friends. But most of all, he's cheering you on, because we all know that you were his favorite."

"I don't know about that," Kingston mumbled.

"No, but I do."

The funeral service was zipping by but then froze when Rustic got up to speak. He tugged uncertainly at his suit jacket sleeve. His hair was flattened oddly against his head since he wasn't wearing his normal camouflage ball cap. His voice quivered as he spoke.

"I'll never forget Juan Sebastian. I needed a job after the war, and he gave me one. Boy, was I a mess. I was in a drunken stupor every night. He didn't judge me. He talked to me. He helped me to see beyond the pain. It led to AA and now I'm twenty-six years sober. Not great with words. Guess the best way to say it is that he was a very good man because of all the little things he did when no one was looking."

As soon as the service ended, Jude disappeared. Kingston knew his brother didn't want to get emotional in front of anyone.

Kingston sat in a daze as people slowly made their way out of the chapel. He felt a bump on his shoulder and saw his best friend, Cooper.

"Sorry I'm late," he said. "I left right after my last final and drove through the night to get here."

Kingston half smiled. "Energy drink madness."

"Only way to fly. I mean, drive. How's the internship?"

"Challenging."

"I still think it's crazy that you're working for the billionaire of my dreams. You are one lucky dog. What's he like?"

"I don't know how to say it exactly. He brings out the best in you and expects you to show up fully without it being threatening."

"The complete opposite of your dad. What do they got you doing?"

Kingston caught himself and realized he had to paint the story. The story that he had practiced so many times it was as if it were real. "I am working for the foundation. Vetting each candidate like a private investigator to make sure each need is legitimate. It's a lot of grunt work and late hours. Not a lot of time to do much else."

Cooper took the seat next to Kingston and said nothing more until they were the last two sitting in the chapel.

"Ready to say goodbye?" Cooper asked.

"No," Kingston replied.

"All right. I'll wait outside until you are ready." He then got up and left.

Kingston could hardly bring himself to leave, to say his last goodbye. But he finally built up enough courage to bring himself to his feet and take the first step toward the door. He never looked back.

■ ■ ■

The entire family was seated in the lawyer's office for the reading of Papa Juan's will. Franco was camped on one side of the room and Tomas on the other. The two brothers had hardly spoken to each other at the funeral.

Tomas, the appointed executor, read the will out clearly. "I, Juan Sebastian Rais, being of sound mind, do leave the following…"

Kingston's thoughts blocked out Tomas's droning voice. He noticed that Jude had not showed up for the reading, which he thought was really odd. His mind went back to training. He'd been gone four days, but it felt like a lot longer. He wanted to get back, to get away from all this. He wanted to forget. Kingston snapped out of his daydream when he heard his dad calling his name. Kingston mumbled out an apology and found he was moving to where his dad was standing.

Tomas coldly handed him a ring box and said, "Papa Juan wanted you to have this."

Kingston looked stunned. "Me? He's given it to me?" Kingston opened the box and saw the emerald ring staring back at him. "I don't think I can accept this. It belongs to you, Dad."

"No, son. He wanted you to have it. We must respect his wishes," said Tomas a little too sternly.

Kingston knew his dad would resent it for the rest of his life if he took the ring, so he desperately tried to give it back to him. "No, really. He wasn't in his right mind." Kingston tried to place the box into his dad's hand. Tomas batted it away as if it were some pesky insect.

Suddenly, Franco stood up and said, "If neither of you want it, I'll take the ring."

Tomas flared up instantly. "What? So you can sell the soul of our father? You already took his savings, now you want to take his legacy from my son?"

Franco puffed up. "Oh, here we go again. I'll have you know I run a successful business, and I paid back every cent I borrowed from him; however, you wouldn't know that if you had spoken to our father before he died."

Tomas tossed aside the flimsy podium that held the official papers, causing them to fly in all directions, and then like a freight train rushed toward Franco, who was standing behind a chair.

Kingston stealthily sprung in between them. "Listen, I'll take the ring."

Tomas tried to push his son out of the way, but failed to move him, so he yelled over Kingston's shoulder. "Franco, all of this is your fault. You ruined everything. I was supposed to be the one who ran the business. But you took that away from me. You ruined my relationship with him. You had him all starry-eyed with big promises of greatness, and what did you give him in the end? Nothing. You took all he had and gave him nothing."

"Oh, I paid him back in full, with interest. I made my wrong right with him. You, on the other hand, deserted him," said Franco.

Tomas went around Kingston, launching over a chair, and knocked Franco to the ground. Everyone in the room stood up and stared in silence at the two grown men rolling around on the floor.

Kingston went to stop them, but his mom, Margarite, grabbed his arm. "Let them work it out. They have ten years of history to deal with." She then turned to the onlookers and firmly stated, "Everyone, let's move out into the lobby for a few minutes." The open-mouthed group slowly made their way out of the room, peeking back over their shoulders so as not to miss a second.

Twenty minutes later, Tomas and Franco emerged from the room. Tomas had a swollen eye and Franco a bloody nose.

Both seemed to have found some sort of peace. Tomas motioned for everyone to come back into the room. As Kingston passed Tomas, he said, "Sorry about that, Dad. I didn't mean to cause any trouble."

"It's not your fault, son," said Tomas.

The next morning, Kingston waited at the front door for his car to arrive. He was headed back. He checked his watch, hoping that his dad would be home in time from his workout. As if on cue, his dad pulled into the driveway.

Kingston stepped outside onto the porch with his bags in hand. Tomas noticed him and said, "Headed out?"

"Yep, the car should be here shortly," said Kingston.

Tomas coughed and pounded his chest. "Do your best." He then brushed past his son to head inside.

"Dad, I really think you should have this," said Kingston.

Tomas turned around slowly and looked at the ring sitting in Kingston's hand. He moved closer and picked it up, examining it. He then put it back into Kingston's hand.

"This is what Papa Juan wanted," said Tomas.

"No, it isn't. He wanted to give it to you. He thought you would refuse to take it," Kingston said passionately and tried to put the ring into his dad's hand.

Tomas took a step backward. "You were meant to have it. No matter what, we need to respect his final wishes."

"I don't care about his wishes. No ring is worth that," pleaded Kingston.

Tomas reached out and grabbed his son by both shoulders. "He wanted you to have it, not me."

Even as his dad said those words, Kingston wondered what broke between the two of them. Why it always seemed there was some sort of crevice between them. Was it because Kingston reminded him of his brother, Franco? Was it because he didn't measure up to the high expectations he held over him? What was it?

The words tumbled out before he could stop himself. "Then what it is? What did I do to make you hate me so much?" asked Kingston.

"I don't. I know, I don't probably show it the way you want me to. But you matter to me, and you should have the ring."

Kingston moved to hug his dad, but Tomas reached out to shake his hand instead as the car pulled up to the front of the house.

# CHAPTER 31

Lincoln found Kingston in the decompress room. Kingston hadn't said much since he returned from the funeral. According to Dr. Greystone, the only thing she could extract from him was that he didn't want to talk about it. His reaction was classic denial in the stages of grief.

The team was unified in giving Kingston space. However, they had still not come together fully. Sam seemed to be in a hurry to get the team field-ready and had been showing up more often. Lincoln wasn't sure why. Maybe Sam was really getting back to normal. Maybe Sam wanted to take the reins back from him.

Lincoln hoped that his meeting with Sam this morning would be more enlightening. He found Sam in the central hub reviewing Kingston's tapes.

"How's Kingston holding up?" asked Sam.

"Not sure. He's not talking to anyone about it."

Sam paused then said, "Grief is an elusive adversary. You never know when it's going to hit."

Lincoln thought for a moment then asked, "Should I pull him out of rotation?"

"Actually, no. I think the distraction would be good for him until he is ready to confront his feelings."

"Is that what you wanted to meet about?"

"I think we need to toss them in the deep end of the pool with a life jacket."

"How would we do that?"

"I think that they could be useful at the Future Trust Gala."

"Really? How?"

"You know, your mother is the head of the host committee this year and your father would feel more comfortable with added undercover security. From what I hear, they have a few members of royalty attending."

"I don't know if the team would be interested in being security guards."

"We could sweeten the pot and send in a fake threat or two. Just to test their ability in a real-world scenario."

"That could work."

# CHAPTER 32

Kingston entered the central hub for a brief team meeting. He needed a distraction. He felt a heavy cloud of sadness following him, and he didn't want to get caught in an emotional hurricane. Dr. Greystone had cornered him twice; however, he was able to put her at bay by saying he wasn't ready to face his new reality in which Papa Juan was no longer available.

"We are foregoing our normal schedule to go on an excursion," announced Lincoln. "Pack for the weekend. The details of the location are in the planning system. Log in. Wheels up in an hour." He then abruptly left.

When Kingston reached the airstrip, the entire team made their way to the silver-pearl Gulfstream G650 and climbed the short staircase to board.

The interior was white leather with dark-walnut wood accents. It was illuminated with a soft blue glow. Kingston found a seat near a window and planted himself there hoping that no one would ask how he was feeling.

Pandora found a seat next to Kingston and said, "Sorry about what happened."

"It doesn't seem real." Kingston turned his head away from her, holding it all back, and saw Lincoln walking up to the plane pulling his overnight bag behind him.

"Glad your back," Pandora said.

"You might be the only one," Kingston commented as he put in his earbuds and closed his eyes for the flight.

The plane landed on a small private airstrip on the Silas Refuge off the coast of Belize. Four chauffeured golf carts arrived to pick them up.

The head driver said to Lincoln in a thick accent, "Welcome back to Belize, Mr. Silas. Your mother requested that everyone unpack, settle in, and then meet at the main house in three hours.

The golf carts drove along a well-manicured path surrounded by an unruly jungle. The carts broke through a clearing, revealing an expansive, white-columned house nestled in front of a sandy beach. Kingston had never experienced such opulence. He was amazed at the view for a few moments; his wonder making him forget his loss.

Lucky whistled low and high and said what Kingston was thinking, "Brilliant home."

The golf carts continued down the path to a guesthouse that came complete with an infinity pool and an exercise room. Lincoln ushered the team into their shared space and quickly said, "Your names are tagged on the doors of your rooms. Please be at the main house in three hours sharp and be prepared for inspection by my mother, Sofia, and Marco the stylist."

"Did he say *stylist*?" Pandora said.

"Aw, Pandora, are you petrified?" Violet jabbed.

"No change needed here," Lucky said as he motioned to himself.

Roosevelt laughed and shook his head. "You're gonna need the most help."

Kingston wasn't sure what to say. He didn't like the idea of his appearance being judged. He was confused as to why they were here. Wasn't there some terrorist that needed to be found? He quietly walked away and found his room. He dropped his bag and pulled out the ring box. He opened it. His finger slid across the rough part of the emerald. He felt a tear slip down his face. He quickly wiped it away, snapped the box shut, and put it back into his bag.

Exactly three hours later, the team arrived at the main house. They were led by a butler of sorts to a side entrance and deposited in a room that had a platform in the center. The room was sparsely decorated and had full-length mirrors on one side of the room and floor-to-ceiling windows on the other side. Lincoln rushed in and hopped up on the platform.

"Okay, guys. We are going on our first real mission. Every year there is this invitation-only meeting called the Future Trust. It is attended by high-net-worth individuals, politicians, and influencers from all over the world. This year it's being held in Washington, D.C. My mother is president of the host committee for the benefit gala and we've been asked to run an additional layer of security.

Violet rolled her eyes. "We are going to be security guards?"

"No, it's a little more complex. We will function undercover in addition to the visible security and search for any and all threats. In about two minutes my mother will walk through that door. She is going to assess your look and position. Accept whatever she recommends."

Sofia Silas entered the room trailed by her stylist, Marco. Kingston noticed that she was frightfully thin. Her décolletage featured a protruding collarbone and rib cage. A thick gold-leaf chain necklace cleverly placed to distract from the evidence of her lack of eating. Her long flowing white camisole dress compensated for the rest of her skeletal frame. She carefully inspected each person, having each one turn around for her. Her stylist, Marco, with tan skin and a bright smile, followed behind her and took copious notes. Lincoln was quietly perched on a stool in the corner of the room.

"Marco, what do you think of this one?" Sofia remarked as she studied Pandora.

As he lifted up Pandora's hair, Marco replied, "Ah, her cheekbones are everything."

"Okay, I think I'll put her at coat check," stated Sofia. "Make sure her uniform is fitted to perfection."

Marco went to work measuring Pandora's waist. Pandora looked incredibly uncomfortable with some strange man in her personal space.

"Such beautiful skin. I want her eyes to pop, and keep the rest natural. Also, please do something about the color of her hair so that it's more suitable to her skin tone," noted Sofia.

"Agreed. I've got a perfect lip color that would work on her, and I'll make sure that her hair tones are flawless," said Marco.

Pandora's eyes were wide and stared at Lincoln in horror as she lightly touched the strands of white hair around her face. Lincoln shrugged his shoulders and raised his hands as if to say, sorry.

Sofia continued on to Roosevelt and eyed him closely. "What's your name?"

"Roosevelt, ma'am," he said, flashing a toothy smile.

"Decent smile," Sofia commented. "Let's place him at the beginning of the red carpet. We want to show that we take security seriously. Let's dress him in a fitted, two-button black suit, not a uniform. Crisp white shirt. "

Marco nodded. "I know exactly what to put him in."

"And, Roosevelt, don't smile. I prefer that you look serious throughout the evening," said Sofia.

"Certainly, ma'am," said Roosevelt, wiping the smile off his face.

Sofia paused at Lucky and shook her head. "This one needs serious attention."

"Excuse me?" Lucky shot back, shocked at the suggestion.

"Haircut short, a shave, and all visible tattoos need to be covered up," said Sofia.

Lincoln coughed loudly, sending a message to Lucky to shut up and take it.

"Rough canvas. I'll do my best to make him a masterpiece," said Marco.

"Just in case, let's station him as the bartender in that dark corner off the performance hall," said Sofia.

Marco nodded. "Ah yes, good idea. The lighting will be forgiving there."

Sofia continued on and paired Dr. Pharma and Violet together as a guest couple. The stylist reviewed some looks for Violet, and Sofia selected a sparkling gown for her.

As Kingston waited, he noticed the figure of a slender girl with blonde hair walking out to the ocean edge. He wished he was out there and not stuck in this suffocating room.

"Hmm, interesting," Sofia said as she looked Kingston up and down. "He skews a bit young. Good-looking with a friendly face, though. Let's station him as one of the gala photographers and put him in the uniform with the colors of the night."

Kingston smelled alcohol on her breath then started to feel hot all over. He wasn't sure if someone had raised the temperature of the room. Maybe the asthma inhibitor wasn't working. He got his bracelet directly from Dr. Pharma, so Violet couldn't have meddled with it.

Marco did his measurements briskly and continued after Sofia.

He started to feel like he couldn't breathe. He started to feel dizzy. He needed to get out of the room. Kingston stumbled a little, and sweat covered his entire body.

Before Kingston even knew what was happening, Dr. Pharma appeared in front of him and checked his vitals.

"Kingston, take deep breaths," Dr. Pharma ordered.

Kingston inhaled deeply and exhaled slowly. He could breathe.

"I think he needs a break," Dr. Pharma suggested.

"No, I'm fine," Kingston muttered.

"All right, let's break for lunch," Lincoln stated.

"I've given him something to take the edge off, but some fresh air might do him some good."

Kingston lounged on a beach chair and nibbled on a turkey and cheese sandwich. He already felt better. He wanted to take a walk and clear his head. He got up without a word to anyone and walked off.

Kingston disappeared down the path he saw the blonde girl taking down to the edge of the ocean. He reached a cove that housed a cabana. He found the girl sunbathing on the beach.

The beautiful girl's eyes were transfixed on her phone when Kingston said a light "Hello." She jumped and screamed at the same time, tossing her phone to the ground.

"Sorry, didn't mean to scare you," said Kingston.

The girl quickly grabbed for her phone. "Don't come any closer," she said as she pressed a button on her phone. "This island is private. You shouldn't be here."

"I know, I'm here—" Kingston had barely gotten out the words when he was slammed to the ground. Five guys dressed in camouflage had appeared out of nowhere and tackled Kingston to the sand.

Minutes later, Lincoln sprinted up the beach and said in between breaths, "Guys, please, he's with me."

The five guys removed themselves from Kingston, dusted him off, and helped him stand up. They all took off back down the beach.

"Kingston, sorry about that. This is my sister, Genevieve," Lincoln said sheepishly.

Kingston laughed a little. "Now that was an introduction."

"Genevieve, he's with the security team for the gala. Didn't you get mother's email?'

Lincoln scolded.

"No," said Genevieve sharply.

"Perhaps you should read your email occasionally," said Lincoln.

"Doesn't he know that certain parts of the island are off-limits to the help?" asked Genevieve.

"G, stop it," barked Lincoln.

"Stop what?" teased Genevieve.

Lincoln bristled. "Put a leash on your snobbery."

Genevieve rolled her aquamarine eyes and flipped over on her stomach, ignoring them.

Kingston and Lincoln headed back to the house.

"Hey man, I'm sorry. I didn't know that it was off-limits. I wouldn't have—" Kingston started.

"She's being ridiculous," Lincoln replied.

They had walked a little farther down the beach in silence

when Lincoln finally asked, "How you hanging in there?"

"I'm all right," said Kingston.

"Do you need to take some time off?"

"That's the last thing I need."

"I'm the same way. Distract me so I don't have to deal."

"Yep."

Lincoln didn't look at him directly but said, "At some point, your grief will come out. It's important to let it so you can move forward."

Kingston nodded his head in response. He was afraid if he said one word, he would turn into a blubbering mess.

"I gotta run to meet up with my father. Catch ya later?"

Kingston smiled but still said nothing. He watched Lincoln jog off and then sunk down in the sand and let all the tears flow freely.

# CHAPTER 33

Lincoln went to meet his father at the main house. Hunter wanted to talk. Face-to-face meetings meant only one of two possibilities: either Lincoln was in serious trouble, or it was something of the utmost importance. Lincoln thought this might be the precise moment to tell his father he was ready to fully devote himself to Platinum Security Group.

It had truly been his sole focus the past four years and he loved what he did. The truth was that he was already fully invested. He felt as though it would be best for him to own what he had been building under Sam's direction. Maybe even one day he'd take Sam's place at the helm. Maybe that should be now. After all, he had single-handedly run the division while Sam was out taking care of his wife, Esther.

Lincoln found his father in his usual spot on the veranda located off the master bedroom. He grabbed a bottle of imported sparkling water from the outdoor fridge and popped the cap. "You wanted to see me?"

"I would like to talk to you about your future," said Hunter.

"Good. I have some thoughts about that as well."

"I have to say, you've really impressed me as of late," complimented Hunter.

"Thanks," said Lincoln apprehensively bracing himself, because generally a criticism followed any sort of compliment that his father doled out.

"I have to admit to you that after your average results at college, I was uncertain if you were up to the task."

There it was, the famous Hunter compliment that builds you up then smacks you back down.

Hunter continued on, "Lincoln, you've proved me wrong."

Did his father actually admit that he was at fault? Lincoln couldn't recall anytime that his father had done that.

"I would like to groom you to become Titanium Fortress Investment's future CEO," said Hunter.

"I—I thought you had someone else in mind for your job?" Lincoln stammered.

"The loss of Harris really showed me that I need someone truly loyal," Hunter replied.

Lincoln cleared his throat and coughed a little, stood up, and then sat back down. His next move mattered. "I thought that I would be a better fit in the security arm of the company."

"What? No. It was a good place for you to learn how to build and manage teams so you could use that expertise in our real business, not in Sam's intricate hobby of saving the world."

"But numbers make me cross-eyed, and you know I'm terrible at investments," said Lincoln.

"I'll help you, and we'll hire for your weaknesses. In all honesty, you were born to lead this company."

Lincoln sighed. He needed more time and perhaps a way out. He finally replied, "This is such a great responsibility and for certain an honor. I really need a chance to process it thoroughly. Can I have some time to think about it?"

"What's there to think about? This is an invaluable opportunity."

"I can't up and leave. I built this team. They depend on me. They trust me. What would it say for me to jump ship now when we are assimilating a new member? They'll think I'm just another rich-kid opportunist."

"Frankly, I don't care what they think. You need to look at the bigger picture here. We're building a legacy. The greatness that's inside of you will be capped there in that position. This path with TFI will not only give you limitless opportunity, but it will also challenge you to become something better than you are today."

"Please. You understand better than anyone what it's like to build something and own it. You would be devastated if Sam told you that you had to leave and start something new. Please give me some time to think how to best transition to this role."

"I'll give you six months to make the transition," Hunter offered.

"I really need a year or two," Lincoln countered.

"I'll give you nine months. Sam can take it from there."

"Okay," Lincoln accepted. He had bought some time for himself. But was it enough?

Hunter reached out to shake Lincoln's hand. "I know you can't see it right now, but eventually you'll see this is the right move for you."

Lincoln felt like a little boy who had been reprimanded by his father. His mind already spinning on how he could get out of this.

As soon as he left the veranda, Lincoln called Sam. "Did you know about my father's offer?"

"I did."

"Sam, why didn't you fight him? Tell him that I needed to be with the team."

"Because that would've been me overstepping."

"After all I've done for you."

"Listen, I don't want you to go. But it's not my job to fight for you to stay. It's yours."

"You know I don't have a choice."

"There's always a choice, Lincoln."

"I'm going to find a way around this."

"I know you will, son."

# CHAPTER 34

A few days after the excursion to the Silas Refuge, Lincoln quickened his pace down the corridor to the central hub at Atlantic One. His rebellious hand slid along the smooth wall trying to slow him down, trying to slow time down. He still had not come up with a good enough plan to change his father's mind about his future. He couldn't imagine not being here. He never saw his life anywhere else but here.

Kingston whizzed by him, knocking Lincoln out of his thoughts. He hollered, "You're headed in the wrong direction."

"Left my tablet in my room," Kingston yelled back while running at a dead sprint. "And Dr. Pharma will be annoyed if I forget it again."

Lincoln's smile disappeared as he realized he was going to miss all this. He paused at Dr. Greystone's office and popped his head in. She was intently studying a report.

"Hello, Dr. Greystone, do you have a minute?"

Dr. Greystone looked up and smiled. "I wondered when you'd be stopping by."

Lincoln plopped down in a chair. "You heard about my promotion?"

"I did. What an amazing opportunity."

"I guess."

"You want to talk about it?"

"I do and I don't. I'm irritated. Doesn't he get this is what I want to do with my life?" Lincoln got up and grabbed a bottled water from Dr. Greystone's small fridge.

"Lincoln, I've known you since you were little. You've never been a halfway in type of person. You are all in. You fully commit and don't let go. I can understand why it would be difficult to leave all this behind. On the other hand, the opportunity ahead could grant immeasurable possibilities. You have a tough decision to make."

"I don't want to leave," Lincoln said as he squeezed his water bottle then shook it.

"Why's that?" asked Dr. Greystone softly.

"I don't want to work for my father," Lincoln confessed.

"Why not?"

"Because I want something of my own. Not something that's handed to me. That's why I like it here so much. It's all mine."

"Interesting."

Lincoln started to leave and then turned back around. "What's so interesting?'

"Oh, you don't want to hear it, dear."

"Tell me," said Lincoln, followed by a delayed "Please."

"You always limit yourself. You have a grand opportunity to really grow and become something even greater, and yet you want to stay at the kids' table and play with toys. That's fine by me, but I know you'll regret it someday."

"Did Father…er...Mr. Silas pay you to say that?"

She paused for a moment and straightened her cardigan. "You should know by now I'm here to help everyone emotionally manage. I can't be bought."

"Dumb question."

"Didn't you have a meeting that you needed to get to?"

Lincoln returned to the hallway and chucked the water bottle down the hall and watched it roll away like everything else in his life.

■ ■ ■

Lincoln entered the central hub and perched on the desk next to Pandora.

Most of the team had arrived for the pre-gala briefing. As per usual, Kingston was up front and center with tablet in hand. A hoodie-covered Pandora slunk in with an energy drink and managed to land in her turntable chair soundlessly. Dr. Pharma sneezed into his tissue and reluctantly parked in the far-right front seat, still slightly annoyed that Kingston had taken his original space.

Lucky made his grand entrance with high fives all around then found a comfortable spot in the far back corner to spread out. Roosevelt settled smack-dab in the middle of the room, while Violet lounged on top of the desk adjacent to him.

Lincoln shifted uncomfortably. "I'd like to hear status reports."

Violet crossed her arms. "I still don't see why a normal security team couldn't handle this event."

"We've received a few threats that may be nothing, but we need to make sure that this event is completely safe given who is inside the room."

He then leaned over toward Pandora. "Is identification software ready to go, Pan? We need to make sure that each guest who walks through those doors matches the guest list. "

“We will mount several cameras throughout the venue,” Pandora answered.

“All the employees vetted?”

“Most of them. I’m still working through the catering company. They’re still in the process of hiring for some reason.”

“Luck, how are those signature drinks coming?” Lincoln asked.

“I think I’ve missed my calling. The Pink Salty Dog is very tasty.”

“Beyond the drinks, what tools do you have for us?”

Lucky lifted his gloved hands. “I got these brilliant medicated gloves thanks to one of Dr. Pharma’s sweet potions. If you touch any bare skin, the person will take a nice nap for a few hours.

“It also affects the short-term memory. A nice touch if we don’t want to be remembered,” Dr. Pharma added.

Also, I’ve got these dandy little earbuds the size of a dot. They won’t be noticeable at all. They pick up any sound in a ten-foot radius. Lastly, I have these wicked-smart contact lenses that act as night vision, heat vision and a visual messaging system.”

Lincoln then turned to Dr. Pharma. “Doctor, do you have your personal history memorized?”

The doctor coughed then wiped his nose and cleared his throat. “I studied several brain surgeries and have the working language perfected. I love bird-watching. I’m exceptionally fond of the Asian crested ibis. The red-tipped beak is outstanding.”

“Is the tracker mist ready?”

“Yes. When everyone crosses into the lobby, they will pass through a grapefruit-scented mist that will mark them. Pandora will connect the tracker to the ID software, so not only will we know who the person is, but also where they are physically in the building,” replied Dr. Pharma, wiping his nose again.

"Exceptional work, Dr. Pharma and Lucky," Lincoln complimented. "Violet?"

"I got my history down," she responded.

"Care to elaborate?"

"Not really."

"I would appreciate it if you gave us a glimpse."

"I'm in marketing. I work for a virtual closet company that provides the service of putting couture in climate-controlled storage and delivering it to you when you need it."

"Thanks for sharing." Lincoln looked over at Kingston. "You good with the camera?"

"Yeah, been working with it," said Kingston. "Should be all set. I sent you a few snaps to review."

"Good. Roosevelt, how's the additional muscle?"

Roosevelt leaned back. "I got some off-duty lined up. We've got lockdown and evacuation plans set. Consider me ready."

Lincoln knew he had to address the team about his imminent departure at some point. Maybe after the gala.

"Is that all?" asked Violet. "I've got a few things to do before we leave."

Lincoln seemed taken aback by Violet's abruptness. "Yes. That's all." Violet then got up, avoiding his gaze, and left the room. Lincoln turned his attention back to the others. "We are wheels up in the morning. Then we need to lock down the location and set up a security perimeter."

# CHAPTER 35

The entire team arrived in Washington, D.C., after a red-eye flight. Still blurry-eyed, Kingston entered the Kennedy Center from the river terrace. It was almost too much to take in. Hard to believe that he was strolling through the grand foyer in a custom-tailored tuxedo. A wave of sadness passed over him; he wished Papa Juan could see him now.

He reached the long Hall of States and held his camera up to his eye. He used the lens to zoom in and found Pandora at the other end. He almost didn't recognize her clad in a formfitting uniform, her hair dyed black and styled elegantly. He pressed a button on his camera and captured her image then clicked on his earpiece.

"Wow, have you guys checked out Pandora?" asked Kingston.

Pandora twisted around, but didn't see Kingston because he had positioned himself expertly behind an elevated platform set up for the string quartet.

Lucky was first to respond from inside the Opera House. "Such a stunner."

Roosevelt jumped in from outside. "Did she wear her kicks?"

"If you guys don't shut up, I'll personally sell your information on the black market and put you on every no-fly list," threatened Pan.

"Can't you handle a compliment?" Kingston said with a laugh. He then turned around, and before he knew it, Pan was standing right beside him. "Wow, how did you make it here that quick?"

Pan tried to look serious then cracked a slight smile. "No more comments, Rais."

The event manager walked by and said, "Ms. Vu, shouldn't you be at coat check preparing for the guests?"

Pandora smiled sweetly and said, "Yes, I needed to clarify something with Kingston."

The entire team had spent the past two days taking an online etiquette class followed by memory tests on everyone's names. Who knew that the event manager's class would be the toughest part of the assignment?

Pandora dutifully followed the manager back to her station. She turned around and wagged her finger at Kingston. He clicked the shutter and captured Pan's look of reproach.

Kingston found Dr. Pharma setting up the translucent mist at the front entrance where everyone would enter. He was a few feet away from Dr. Pharma, but the doctor did not acknowledge his presence. Kingston had noticed that he was hyper focused while working on a project. At the moment, he was connecting the machine to the pink-tinged liquid. Kingston snapped a picture of Dr. Pharma's determined face then cleared his throat.

Dr. Pharma flicked his eyes up and said, "Perfect timing. Could I have you walk through the mist?"

"Sure," Kingston said as he put the camera down and straightened his suit.

Dr. Pharma clicked his remote and the mist turned on. It couldn't be seen but the slight smell of grapefruit wafted through the air. "Go ahead."

Kingston walked through the invisible mist and felt no moisture at all.

Dr. Pharma radioed, "Pan, did you catch that?"

Over the earpiece, Pan responded, "Kingston has been marked with the fruit, but I can't see him."

"That's because the ghost-ware is in play," Lucky chimed in.

"What's the ghost-ware?" Kingston asked.

"Oh, it's just a little invention that I created. That boutonniere you're wearing blocks your image from being captured. It's like you're a ghost."

"Where's the camera?" Kingston asked.

Dr. Pharma pointed to the soft illuminating light positioned just above their heads. "Decorations always provide the necessary line of sight."

He waved his hand, "So, you guys can't see me?"

Pandora replied, "No. We can see the chemical, though, so we know where you're positioned."

Kingston pushed air out of his lungs. He was nervous. This was his first real live mission. He wanted everything to go smoothly. He continued to stroll around the venue noting good lighting and locations to take great photographs. He wasn't paying attention and ran directly into Violet. He had to do a double take. She was already very attractive, but somehow her beauty was elevated even more, like she had stepped off the cover of a fashion magazine.

"Hey, mind if I take your picture?"

"Actually, I do mind."

"You, um, look nice."

"I better after five hours of being stuck in a room."

Violet looked past him as Lincoln walked up to the pair.

"I'm headed out to arrive with my parents. Remember it's of utmost importance that you don't show any sign of recognition when you see me."

Kingston hadn't thought of that and filed that information in his brain.

Violet responded, "That will not be a problem."

"Why are you being so harsh?" asked Lincoln.

Kingston studied his shoes trying to think of some way he could excuse himself from this uncomfortable conversation.

"You should know why," Violet responded.

"I don't," Lincoln said as he headed to the exit.

Violet turned on her heel and didn't say another word to Kingston.

Kingston commented to himself, "That was fun."

He lifted his camera and took a full-length picture of Violet walking away.

■ ■ ■

Kingston positioned himself out on the red carpet. He watched as town cars filled the two half-circle driveways, unloading accomplished individuals that represented old money, new money, tech money, and government money. Jewels dripped, couture waltzed, and everything screamed expensive. Guests with security entourages filed down the red carpet while the press documented their entrances.

The Silas family was fashionably late. Hunter wore a custom tuxedo and his bow tie perfectly matched the shade of Sofia's delicate pink gown. Then Kingston caught sight of Genevieve. Her hair was softly pulled up in a messy bun and her dress was hanging elegantly on her thin frame. She confidently stepped along the red carpet with some good-looking, young man by her side. Lincoln followed behind with no one on his arm. They appeared to be the perfect family.

Kingston peered through the lens of his camera and took pictures of the last trickle of guests arriving on the red carpet. He noticed Roosevelt intently observing the late arrivals. Nobody was messing with him tonight.

Kingston circled behind the building and entered through the employee door in the back. He wandered past a group of waiters huddled around trays of crudités. He pushed into the main lobby and continued to photograph various couples and groups of people. He scanned the crowd and caught a glimpse of Dr. Pharma and Violet. When Violet walked through the crowd, he watched several men gape at her as their dates glared. She certainly was the ultimate distraction. He moved his lens along and found Lucky mixing and shaking away while making small talk.

From his vantage point, the night was going smoothly.

# CHAPTER 36

Lincoln observed the lobby. He watched as the remainder of the guests passed through the elaborate security checkpoint, where bags were checked and bodies were scanned by a machine that also recorded DNA. Dr. Pharma's translucent, grapefruit-scented mist tagged each person as they walked through the front door. Pan had set the program to take an image from entry, match it with the person's DNA, and funnel it through her identity authentication software to verify that people were who they said they were before they even reached the coat check.

Lincoln deftly moved through the crowd without a date. Many surprised conversations ignited as the eligible bachelor passed by. It was unusual for Lincoln not to have the latest socialite on his arm. He paused for pictures and brilliantly smiled.

Lincoln then strategically found the biggest investor at Titanium Fortress Investments, Edward Pearce. "Hello, Mr. Pearce, so good to see you here tonight."

"Lincoln, where have you been hiding? I've missed you on the golf course," said Mr. Pearce.

"Oh, you know, I've been working hard behind the scenes. I hope to join you very soon."

"You better. Your father is a great CEO, but his game isn't the challenge I need."

Lincoln laughed, "All right. I'll reach out soon. Did I hear your son, Simon, was player of the year for the Big 12 and only a junior? Congratulations!"

"Yes, and thank you. His diligent training paid off. We're very proud of him."

Lincoln then noticed Pandora out of the corner of his eye. "Please, if you'll excuse me. I need to check on my mother."

Mr. Pearce's eyes twinkled. "Hope to see you on the green soon."

"Absolutely, Mr. Pearce."

When Lincoln reached coat check, he asked Pandora, "Miss, could you direct me to the terrace? I need to make a quick call."

Pandora smiled. "It's down the hall straight through those doors." Her reply was code that everything was going well. Lincoln left the coat check and ran into Mr. and Mrs. Chadwick.

"Oh hello, Lincoln," said Mrs. Chadwick.

"Hello, Mrs. Chadwick. You look stunning. Did you do something new with your hair?" Lincoln replied.

Mrs. Chadwick blushed then chattered, "How do you do that? You always notice the little things. Oh, I was so hoping to introduce to our daughter, Eleanor. She planned to be here tonight, but somehow she missed her flight."

"I'd love to meet her," said Lincoln warmly. "How was your flight over the pond?"

"Horrible landing," coughed out Mr. Chadwick, who was known for using his words economically.

"We were on two wheels for a second or two. But the pilot got us safely to the gate. What a lovely evening this is! How does your mother continue to outdo herself each year?" Mrs. Chadwick cut-in.

"My mother is talented, but I'm biased. I'm glad that you arrived safely," said Lincoln. He then spotted his mother waving him over. "Now, if you'll excuse me, Mother is calling."

"Certainly," said Mrs. Chadwick. Lincoln overheard her say as he walked off, "August, I really like that boy. He could be a good option for our Eleanor."

"Eleanor's not ready for marriage," said Mr. Chadwick as he straightened his tie.

Lincoln made it across the room to find his mother had already been called away. So, he joined his father and Sam perched at a high table.

"Hey, Sam," Lincoln said as he extended his hand.

"Lincoln, it's been a while. I hope you've been well."

"All good."

Lincoln noticed Kingston roving through the crowd and signaled him over,

"Would you mind taking our picture?"

"I'd be happy to, sir." Kingston took the picture, nodded his head, and continued on.

"How's your new employee shaping up?" Hunter asked as Kingston moved out of earshot.

"Better than expected, actually," Sam replied. "He has made great strides with the team."

"Glad to hear," Hunter replied.

Sam reached into his coat pocket, pulled out an envelope, and placed it into Hunter's hand. "I hate to give and run. But I've got a meeting tonight on the West Coast."

Hunter looked surprised. "Really? Who with?"

"Another investor interested in the foundation."

"Who knew retirement would be so exciting?"

"I should go. Give my best to Sofia."

"I will, Sam."

Sam turned and disappeared into the crowd, passing by Pandora on his way out.

Hunter and Lincoln didn't speak a word to each other.

"That reminds me. Your mother wanted you to meet her backstage in about fifteen minutes," Hunter said.

Lincoln turned to go, and Hunter grabbed his arm. "I know this is hard for you. But I promise you will look back and discover that this decision is the best for your future."

Lincoln smiled and then walked off. "I don't think it's best."

# CHAPTER 37

A short tune played in Kingston's ear signaling that a red flag had entered the building. A red flag meant a guest posed as a possible threat. This threat needed to be assessed and removed if necessary.

Pandora's voice whispered in his ear, "We have a problem. Grantor Habesha does not look like Grantor Habesha."

"Did he have some work done?" Violet lightly asked.

"Not unless he's completely changed nationalities from Norwegian to Ethiopian and grew six inches."

"Haven't heard of that procedure," Roosevelt commented.

"Kingston, you should be the closest. He's near Sofia. I'm sending you a few images of him to your lenses. "

The images appeared, and Kingston scanned the room then found Sofia. He searched around her and found a bald, sharp-featured gentleman that stood six foot six. He towered over his five-foot-nothing, petite date.

Flanked by three bodyguards, the couple didn't seem to notice anyone around them. They only had eyes for each other in spite of their height difference.

"They are headed to coat check," said Kingston.

"Lucky, I need two drinks in a hurry and add something

special to both their drinks. Kingston, stay with them," Pandora instructed.

Kingston inconspicuously shadowed the entourage, momentarily stopping to photograph people around him so as not to look obvious. When the couple reached coat check, Kingston stood a measured distance away.

Within a minute, Lucky arrived at the coat check with two pink drinks on his tray.

"Ah, Mr. Habesha, good evening. We've upgraded your seats to a private box. If you'll follow me, I'd like to show you where you will be seated this evening. I've got to signature drinks for you, compliments of our hosts," offered Lucky.

Mr. Habesha looked pleased and handed one drink to his date and took one for himself. They clinked glasses and sipped lightly. Lucky led them down the Hall of Nations to a small doorway that took them to the box.

"Dr. Pharma, how long until the drinks take effect?" asked Kingston.

"Three minutes," Dr. Pharma replied.

Kingston trailed at a distance. Roosevelt caught up with him. "Let's use our gloves." Quickly, they both slid the gloves on, careful not to touch anything.

When they reached the private box away from the eyes of the crowd, Mr. Habesha and his guest stumbled, and the bodyguards tried to help them. Kingston and Roosevelt slipped behind the three bodyguards and quickly touched each one of their necks, causing them immediate unconsciousness.

"We need clean up in Box 104," Roosevelt announced.

Kingston returned to the main floor. He continued sifting through the crowd and took another picture of an elegantly dressed couple. He pushed the autofocus and it somehow focused on the bartender behind them. He noticed him pouring a small tube of pink liquid into a glass, mixing the drink, and then handing it to an overweight, red-cheeked gentleman whose jacket buttons were about to come undone. He continued on through the crowd, where he caught another glimpse of Genevieve. Kingston watched as a man with wisps of white hair barely covering his head walked up behind her.

From his vantage point, he noted that she rolled her eyes at her date. The young man smiled in response and shrugged his shoulders. By the time she turned around to face the older man, a curated smile had appeared on her face. Kingston stepped closer to the table and caught their conversation.

"Oh hello, Senator Kampt. It's so lovely to see you."

"How's my little Evie?" Kampt asked.

"Have I introduced my boyfriend, Benjamin?" she said as her polite smile widened.

The senator extended his hand. "I don't believe so."

Benjamin clasped and shook Kampt's hand firmly then courteously reminded him by saying, "Actually, we met at last year's election fundraiser. "

"Oh yes, now I recall you," the senator replied, somehow managing to get in between them. "You've got a catch there. I've known her since she was little. Do you remember that time when I taught you how to play chess, Evie?"

"Would you mind if I took a photo?" Kingston asked.

Genevieve looked relieved then grabbed the senator's arm and said, "Let's make a permanent memory, shall we?"

"Wonderful, dear."

Genevieve posed expertly, and as soon as the camera came

down from the photographer's face, she locked eyes with Kingston. She then turned and told the senator that her mother needed her and Benjamin before she hit the stage. Kingston continued on meandering through the crowd.

Another tune played across Kingston's earpiece followed by an announcement from Pandora: "Kingston and Dr. Pharma, we have a lady out on the terrace who has something in her purse. I reviewed the bag scan twice, and something's not right. Her name is Harriet Onu."

Kingston pushed through the glass door, assessing the people smoking on the terrace. He found Harriet Onu. She was sipping a pink drink and scrolling through her phone.

"She works for a weapons manufacturing company as their CFO."

A seemingly drunk Dr. Pharma arrived carrying a scotch and pulled out his own vape device that used scented water instead of tobacco. Dr. Pharma sidled up next to Harriet Onu.

"My wife would kill me if she caught me out here," Dr. Pharma said.

Harriet smiled and nodded her head, not wanting to chat.

Pandora spoke over both earpieces, "I checked her social media account and she has a message that says: I HATE FUNDRAISERS. TOO MUCH SMALL TALK. HAVE TO BE HERE UNTIL TEN."

Dr. Pharma tried again. "I can't stand fundraisers."

Harriet turned to him. "I completely agree."

Dr. Pharma got more and more animated as they chatted, then he pressed his vape device to spray Harriet Onu's face with a medicated sedative. Harriet stumbled and Dr. Pharma caught her. Kingston sidled up next to Harriet and escorted her back inside. Once inside, Kingston picked her up and carried her to a room. Dr. Pharma reached into her purse and pulled out a device. He looked at the white oval device. As soon as he touched it, Sam and Lincoln appeared. "Congratulations, team. You successfully completed our hidden threats."

Back in the lobby, Kingston heard a scuffle behind him and traveled quickly in the direction of the noise until he found the large man he had seen earlier completely intoxicated. The additional security team was quietly attempting to remove him from the room without causing a scene.

"Sir, could you please come with us?" a security guard asked calmly.

The large man took an unsteady step and put his fat finger in the guard's chest. "I'm not going anywhere. I got a lot of money to give tonight, and you need me here." He slurred as his voice grew louder and louder.

The lights dimmed in the lobby three times, signaling to the crowd that the main event was about to begin. The guests slowly made their way into the Opera House. Kingston noticed Sofia, who had stopped for a drink at the same bar that the large, boisterous man had visited. Violet and Dr. Pharma were among the last couples to take their seats. Roosevelt worked with the security team to take the large man outside.

Once the crowd was settled, Kingston stood along the back wall as Sofia stepped onto the stage. "Welcome, everyone, to the Future Trust Gala. Tonight, we have the world-renowned soprano Maricella Comolia to entertain us. Remember, you can use your phone during the performance to pledge your donation on the Future Trust app as well as bid on the silent auction."

"Hey, everyone except Violet and Dr. Pharma, come to the

media control room. The stairwell is located next to the east doors," Lincoln said over the comm.

Kingston arrived at the small room with the best view located above Opera House. He scrolled through the evening's images on his camera, pausing on those of Genevieve, while Lucky spun his bottle opener around his finger.

"From my perspective, I call tonight a win," Lincoln warmly said.

# CHAPTER 38

Pan's phone whistled and she clicked it off without looking at it.

"I wanted to take a few minutes to say that you did an incredible job finding the potential threats. Sam and I wanted to give you a real-world scenario for us to see your skills, and you all performed at your best," Lincoln said.

Pan's phone whistled again then began to chirp incessantly. She picked it up and observed the information on the screen. She then held up a finger, not sure which way to point. "Guys, there's a foreign signal going off in the performance hall." She immediately pulled out her laptop and typed at a furious pace. "There are multiple bank transactions happening."

Lincoln waved it off. "Donations are being made by mobile devices throughout the night."

"The amounts are astronomical," said Pandora.

"Really? Mother will be ecstatic," said Lincoln as he walked over to get a peek of the Opera House through the tiny window of the media control room. He looked down and saw the waitstaff in ominous gas masks and all the guests in complete chaos.

Lincoln clicked his comm. "Violet, can you hear me? Dr. Pharma?"

Violet's slurred words came back: "Could you stop yelling in my ear?"

"Okay," Lincoln replied. "Where is Dr. Pharma?"

"Crawling on the floor," Violet replied.

"Can you get him out into the lobby?"

"Yeah, I can."

"Without being seen?"

"Seriously, what is your problem?" Violet started laughing. "Can't you see that I'm in love with you?"

Lincoln stopped talking. Everyone in the control room acted as though they didn't hear the conversation that was going directly into their ears. He then replied, "Could you please get Dr. Pharma to the lobby?"

"I already said yes!"

"What door are you coming out of?"

"The left one."

"East or west?"

"West."

"Also, avoid anyone with a mask."

"Pan, get me eyes and ears in the Opera House. Focus on the west doors. We need to find out what we are dealing with. Open up Dr. Pharma's and Violet's earpieces so I can hear everything."

Pan switched to all the drone feeds they had placed in the room. They were camouflaged in the floating luminescent globes near the ceiling.

All of them viewed Violet as she stumbled past a couple making out in the aisle then got down on all fours next to Dr. Pharma, who was examining something in the carpet.

The doctor held it up and grinned. "I think this will help me cure cancer."

"Hey, we have to go to the lobby," Violet said. "Lincoln wants to talk to you."

"Violet, can't you see that I'm doing serious work here?"

"Yes, I can, and I swear I will return you to your research. But Lincoln needs us right now. Why am I dizzy?"

Dr. Pharma reached up and felt her head and cheeks. "No, you're good."

"Follow me."

Dr. Pharma and Violet crawled in a zigzag line down the back aisle. Before they reached the west door, she saw a masked waiter standing guard.

"Listen, I'm going to tackle the guard, and you go through the door to the lobby," Violet whispered to Dr. Pharma. "Lincoln needs you."

Violet dove at the waiter's feet, knocking him to the ground, as Dr. Pharma clumsily made his way out the door on all fours.

Once through the door, Lincoln grabbed Dr. Pharma up by the arms and dragged him to his feet. "What are they putting in the air?"

Dr. Pharma chuckled at Lincoln. "Oxygen that smells sweet."

"Doc's gone crazy," Roosevelt commented.

Lincoln went at it another way. "What is that sweet smell?"

A puzzled look appeared on Dr. Pharma's face. "Hmmm, that's a really good question, and to answer I would need my spherical sensor. Does the word 'spherical' sound funny to you?"

"It does. Where would I find that sensor?"

"In the yellow case in the van."

Kingston didn't wait for Lincoln to say a word. He dashed out the employees' entrance to where the black van that held their equipment was parked.

"Pandora, I need a head count of how many waiters we have and how many weapons are in the room."

Pandora studied the balloon drone feeds and said, "It looks like we have fifteen. Nine on the main floor. Two on box tier. Two on balcony tier one. Two on balcony tier two. Seven of which are armed with semi-automatic guns."

"How in the world did that much firepower pass us by? Roosevelt, gather the security team from outside. We need as much muscle as we can get."

Roosevelt saluted and jogged to the entrance.

Lincoln turned to Lucky. "Get all the waiter attire in the kitchen. I know the event manager would've ordered ten extras."

"On it," Lucky said as he took off running.

Minutes later, Kingston arrived with the case in hand. Dr. Pharma was again crawling on the floor.

Kingston came down to his level. "What do I do with the spherical sensor?"

Dr. Pharma rolled the ball around and around in his hands. He kept trying to press a button. He finally found it, unsteadily pressed it, and shoved the ball into Kingston's face. "Roll it. Bowl it. Chuck it into the room."

Kingston turned to Pandora. "Any idea where I can access the room without being seen?"

"Let's see, it looks like the east entrance has only one waiter about fifteen feet from the door. I can send you the image of where he's at so you can roll it in when he's not looking," she replied.

Kingston put on his nose plugs and raced off to the Hall of Nations at full speed.

Lincoln sat on the floor with Dr. Pharma, who kept crawling

in circles around him picking up lint. The screen in his hand powered up signaling the sphere had been activated. Lincoln placed the screen in front of Dr. Pharma to show him all the chemical properties in the room.

"There's something in the air in there. Does the word 'air' sound weird to you?" asked Dr. Pharma.

"Any idea what it is?" Lincoln questioned.

"It's like a rooffie."

"What's that?"

"Come on, can't you see it's an airborne Rohypnol," Dr. Pharma said as he pushed the tablet aside and continued to search the carpet for more lint.

Lincoln crawled next to him. "Do you have something to counter it?"

"You should know this! We need lots of oxygen and charcoal."

Lincoln hopped up. "Pan, check his bag and give him what he needs to come back down to planet Earth."

Roosevelt was the first to return with the report. "It seems as though our security has been dosed and all of them are sound asleep."

Lucky arrived with several uniforms in hand and started passing them out to everyone as a winded Kingston showed up next to them.

Kingston, Lincoln, Roosevelt, and Lucky huddled around the virtual map of the Opera House on Pan's computer.

Lincoln tapped the side of his cheek with his index finger and said, "We need to get this situation under control. We need a diversion. Any thoughts?"

"Maybe we should kill the lights?" Lucky offered.

"The devices glow, so there will be some light," Pandora responded.

"But the big question is will they fire their guns?" Roosevelt asked.

Lucky's eyes lit up with excitement as he said, "We could always create a tremor to throw everything off-balance and flicker the power with this nifty machine I've been working on."

"Do you mean create an earthquake?" asked Roosevelt.

"More like the illusion of one. All I would do is use sound to create a vibration on the floor joists of the room using a frequency that's not audible to human ears."

Roosevelt chuckled and said, "And you just happened to bring this new device on this trip?"

"Truth be told, I've been looking for a way to use one of my new inventions," Lucky admitted.

"Pan, do you have architectural drawings of the Opera House?" Lincoln asked.

"I don't, but I can get them."

"Roosevelt, clear the first and second balcony tiers. Kingston, you clear the box tier. Once Lucky has set off the earthquake then all three of you secure the main floor and get my sister and her boyfriend. I'll enter backstage, get my parents, and meet you there."

Lincoln had barely finished speaking when a wobbly Violet arrived at coat check. "Hello, everybody."

"Violet, stay here with Pandora. She will work to get you sober," Lincoln said.

"I will not. I'm going with you."

"I think it'd be better if you stayed."

"What you think is not better."

Roosevelt walked up behind her and clamped a medicated gloved hand on her bare shoulder. Violet immediately lost consciousness, and he caught her in his arms.

Roosevelt held back a laugh and said, “Thought this might be helpful.”

He then carried her over to where Pan was giving Dr. Pharma charcoal and oxygen.

All right, guys, let’s clear the balconies, and Lucky, let us know when you have set off your earthquake.”

“Roger that. Fire power?” said Lucky.

“At this point, let’s use the medicated gloves, tranquilizer guns, and nose plugs. We cannot afford a fatality at this point. Remember, we are ghosts. Leave no DNA behind,” Lincoln added.

“Let’s do this,” said Roosevelt.

# CHAPTER 39

Kingston quietly made his way up the stairs to the box tier. He waited breathlessly outside the door as he asked Pandora to give him confirmation on the location of the two waiters. Pan communicated that the first waiter was positioned by the door he was about to go through and thankfully was distracted by a couple demanding a fresh drink. Kingston crept up behind and touched the back of the waiter's neck, and he went down immediately. Kingston caught the waiter and laid him on the floor. He grabbed the waiter's gas mask and put it on then took the waiter's previous position. The couple looked befuddled, not sure what to say, until the woman finally said, "Maybe we aren't that thirsty after all."

Kingston watched the other waiter located on the opposite side of him strolling along the edge of the tier. He speculated what the best plan of attack would be in order to take him out of the equation.

There was some sort of commotion on the main floor that worked in his favor, and Kingston aimed his tranquilizer gun at the waiter's neck. The tranquilizer dart sunk into his neck causing the waiter to drop to the floor. The box was clear, so Kingston peered over the edge to observe what was happening on the main floor.

The melee of guests continued to trip and fall all over themselves. Some of the guests had fallen asleep. The waitstaff continued up the aisles one row at a time. They appeared to be halfway through the crowd. They were using some sort of scanner to access bank accounts linked to the chip-based cards in the room.

Lucky worked quickly to place the small square sound boxes on the floor. He was also dressed as a waiter and the only way that Kingston could identify him was by the color of his hair. Kingston placed himself as a sniper above everyone, ready to pull the trigger as soon as the lights went out.

# CHAPTER 40

Lincoln stood offstage. He observed his parents sitting on the floor having an argument.

The lights flickered and a rumble ripped through the ground floor of the Opera House and the entire room went black. Lincoln's contact lenses switched to night vision and he stepped onto the stage.

Lincoln picked up his mother, covered her mouth, and carried her offstage. He gently put her down. Sofia had tears streaming down her face. "This is a complete disaster."

Lincoln comforted her. "Don't worry, Mother. I've got this under control."

Lincoln made his way back into the darkness and grabbed his father's arm and whispered in his ear, "Quietly come with me." He led his father offstage and placed him next to his mother.

"Pan, come get my parents and take them to the van. We need to get them treated. They cannot be seen in this state."

Sofia then yelled, "Hunter, the event is ruined, and I blame you."

"Really? You think I had anything to do with this," Hunter replied.

Lincoln headed back onstage and reached for one of the

waiters, making him crumple to the ground. Lincoln dragged the waiter offstage just as the lights flickered for a few seconds, then went completely dark again.

# CHAPTER 41

Kingston expertly shot one waiter then another with his tranquilizer gun. He was silently thankful for all the hours he booked in training to help him nail consecutive targets.

He watched Lucky slyly touch one of the waitstaff in the center aisle and scurry underneath the box tier out of sight. Roosevelt followed suit and snuck behind one of them and the waiter collapsed to the ground.

The lights popped back on and the waiters noticed some of their own missing. The waiter who seemed to be in charge aimed his gun at the ceiling and fired, sending screams throughout the room.

Lucky's device went off a second time, sending a vibration through the room and making the lights go out again. Suddenly, they came back on just as Roosevelt reached out to touch a waiter from behind, and in the confusion, he didn't see the additional waiter behind him.

A male voice yelled, "Hey! What are you—"

Kingston cut him short by sending a dart into his neck.

All heads turned in Roosevelt's direction, and a gun fired several times. The launch of the bullets sent the crowd into pandemonium. Kingston ducked down as a stray bullet whizzed past his head. He looked down just as a waiter fired his gun and hit Genevieve, knocking her to the ground. Kingston saw that she was about to be trampled, and he launched himself off the balcony, accidentally landing on the Senator and knocking him to the ground. He hurdled the rows to reach Genevieve before the stampede of guests crushed her.

When Kingston reached her, he pulled her into the nearby row of seats, barely dodging a rush of feet. He clicked his comm. "Genevieve's been shot."

Lincoln yelled over the comm, "Pan, contact the private hospital. Where's Dr. Pharma?"

Pan responded, "Asleep."

"Wake him up. Pan, get a camera drone on her now. Kingston, where are you?"

"Row 25. Section B."

"How does she look?" Lincoln said.

Kingston looked at the blood seeping through her dress. He noticed that her skin color had turned ashen, and she seemed to be struggling to breathe.

"Not good."

Genevieve looked at Kingston. "It's you. I know you. Am I asleep? Is this real? I have to say, I like you. I can't seem to breathe."

Kingston gently moved her hair out of her face. "It's going to be okay."

The drone flew overhead, and Dr. Pharma said over the comm, "Kingston, do you see an exit wound?"

Kingston gently lifted Genevieve up and saw blood on her back. "Yes."

"That's good. It could be her left lung. Put her on her side to help her breathe with the one good lung. We need to get her out of there."

Genevieve passed out completely.

Unexpectedly, Genevieve's boyfriend clocked Kingston in the jaw. The shock of the punch caught Kingston off guard. He reacted instinctively by throwing a punch back with his gloved hands, which knocked Benjamin out cold.

"Guys, um, I may or may not have knocked Benjamin unconscious."

"Who is Benjamin?" asked Pandora.

"Genevieve's boyfriend," said Kingston.

"Sucks to be you, bro," Roosevelt added. "I'm coming to help you out."

# CHAPTER 42

Back on the main floor, Lincoln craned his neck to see Roosevelt and Kingston carry Genevieve and her boyfriend, Benjamin, out the back of the Opera House.

He jumped up onstage to get a better vantage point and saw the last two of the waitstaff take off running in different directions. Lucky reloaded his tranquilizer gun, aimed at the one who shot Genevieve, and hit him directly in the hand.

Lincoln wasted no time chasing after the last of the counterfeit waitstaff. He caught up to the fleeing waiter and slammed the small-framed person off their feet. Lincoln yanked off the waiter's mask to reveal the scared face of a twenty-year-old girl. He pulled her to her feet. "What is wrong with you? You think you can attack my family and get away with it?"

"They said no one would get hurt. I didn't know that the guns were real, I promise. Please don't turn me in," wailed the girl.

"You should've considered that before agreeing to be a part of it," said Lincoln as he yanked her behind him and strode toward the main doors.

As several police cars surrounded the building, Lincoln clicked his comm. "We need to head out. Pandora, get ahold of one of the waiter devices and reverse all the charges."

"On it," Pandora said.

"King, how's Genevieve doing?"

"She's pale. The medical team is here. They are transporting her off site."

"Okay, stick with her. I don't want her to be alone."

"Will do."

"Roosevelt, do you have Violet, Dr. Pharma, and my parents?"

"Yes, sir!"

"Get them to our van and follow the medical team."

"Lucky, we have a private car out back. It has a secured wireless hub. Take Pandora with you. Then I need you to set up a secured perimeter around the private hospital until Silas Security can get back on their feet."

"Roger that," Lucky said.

Outside, Lincoln made his way through the sea of people. The parking lot had been converted into a makeshift recovery room. Cots were lined up and emergency paramedics were treating bruises and scratches. Some guests were curled up asleep on the steps, and others were failing at having a normal conversation. Lincoln found the police commander near the front doors.

"Hello, sir, I'm Lincoln Silas. Our security team was able to apprehend all the waitstaff who were terrorizing our guests. The majority of the waitstaff have been sedated, but this one is ready to talk." Lincoln then handed off the girl, who was sobbing uncontrollably.

Lincoln sucked in all his emotion and channeled it. He put on a determined face. If there was one thing his father had taught him, it was to use emotion as a tool rather than be ruled by it.

# CHAPTER 43

After leaving the Kennedy Center, the entire team made their way to a small, exclusive hospital. It had an elite membership for only the well-to-do who wanted to keep all health procedures private and out of the press.

The team was running on little sleep. Dr. Pharma and Violet were recovering in the van with IVs stocked full of vitamins to replenish their systems.

Kingston and Pandora stood guard outside the surgical waiting room. Both of them were struggling to stay awake. Pandora somehow found her way back into street clothes and was intently glued to her tablet. She had tapped into the security cameras and monitored all the entrances and exits. Kingston stood up, stretched his arms, and shook his body. Roosevelt was downstairs getting coffee simultaneously checking the halls, and Lucky was perched on top of the building watching everyone around the perimeter.

From what they heard, Genevieve was still in surgery with a top surgeon flown in an hour ago from Florida.

Lincoln appeared and was nervously pacing back and forth in the hallway. His bow tie was hanging loosely around his neck and his top two buttons were undone.

"How did we miss this threat? Did anyone check the waitstaff?"

Pandora sat up and said, "I contacted the caterer. Apparently, there was a flu outbreak with the staff. The event manager hired new people but kept the vetted identities the same. So we were none the wiser."

Lincoln slammed his hand against the wall. "I was so focused on the fake attacks that I never expected that anything else was awry. I didn't see it coming, and now my sister may—"

"She's gonna pull through, man," said Kingston.

Lincoln abruptly turned away and walked down the hall while he said, "I need to check on my parents."

On a flat-screen TV flickered the remnants of the news story about the unfortunate gala events, but it left out the part about anyone being injured. Lincoln had turned the attack into a rescue mission and highlighted the security measures of the event. He also had mentioned that all the money had already been returned to its rightful owners because of their incredible IT team.

Roosevelt entered from outside carrying cups of coffee. He passed them out to Kingston and Pandora. "Any word on G?"

Pandora shook her head and gratefully sipped the hot coffee.

Kingston rubbed his hands together nervously. "She's been in surgery for three hours."

"Hope this has a happy ending. If it doesn't, we could be disassembled," Roosevelt muttered.

That thought made Kingston even more nervous. "Really?" He couldn't sit still any longer. He needed fresh air. The walls were pushing in on him. He abruptly stood up and said, "I'll take the coffee to Lucky."

Roosevelt put on a tired grin and said, "Thanks, my man."

Kingston almost ran down the hallway to the elevator. The

elevator took a long time to arrive and the doors slowly opened. He stepped on and pushed the button to the roof. When he reached the top, he greedily breathed in the fresh morning air. He found Lucky on the front corner. He was lying flat on the ground with a sniper gun and pouring a bottle of water over his head.

Kingston laughed out loud, and it felt good to let it all out.

Lucky peered over his shoulder. "Tell me you got a triple-shot latte."

Kingston held up the coffee cup, and Lucky sighed with relief, saying, "Sadly, I may have closed my eyes for a second or two."

Within minutes of the sun rising in the east, the Silas security guards arrived taking their positions. Lucky and Kingston made it back down to the ground floor.

Dr. Pharma and Violet arrived looking surprisingly refreshed. They all moved down to the cafeteria to wait for the results of Genevieve's surgery.

A disheveled Lincoln appeared. "The surgery was successful. She'll have an intense recovery, though."

# CHAPTER 44

Two hours into his flight, Sam had dozed off.

The stewardess lightly touched his shoulder to wake him, telling him the captain received a message that Sam should check the live-stream news.

Sam quickly sat up and opened up his computer to see complete chaos surrounding the Kennedy Center. He quickly dialed Hunter, but it went directly to voice mail. Same with Lincoln.

"Have them turn the plane around," Sam told the stewardess.

"I will inform the pilot, sir."

Suddenly, the live stream on his computer went black, and a countdown appeared on his screen. It displayed: 90 days | 2160 hours | 129,600 minutes and the phrase *Time to Play*.

# CHAPTER 45

Two days later, Kingston found himself alone at a table. It wasn't any table. It was a table of privilege. A table he never imagined that he would ever be at, but here he was catapulted into a world that he never guessed in his wildest dreams he would be in. He closed his eyes and inhaled the scent of leather meshed with a sweet remnant of pipe smoke. He heard the clinking of ice in glasses, the fire crackling, and the hum of conversation in the next room.

During dinner it was the first time he felt like he was part of a team. It had to be the laughter that brought them even closer together. Lucky was recounting the events of the gala and had everyone literally beside themselves with tears streaming down their faces. Even Violet almost smiled at him. Everything felt right for the very first time in his life.

He opened his eyes and studied the white tablecloth. It was clear of any crumbs thanks to the waiter who pulled out a crumb scraper and removed every speck. The candlesticks had shortened since his arrival. He pushed his hand into his pocket and pulled out his Papa Juan's ring box. He flipped it open. He stared at the ring and wondered if he deserved to wear this family heirloom. He helped save a girl's life, but was that enough? He was certain

Papa Juan would think so. His dad on the other hand would find something wrong.

Lincoln entered the room. "Hey, you joining us?"

Kingston shut the ring box and put it in his pocket. "Yeah, just taking a minute."

"I know, right? It's a lot. Good thing you're made for this. Come on, we're about to do the toasts."

Kingston got up from the table to join the others in the next room. He pulled out the ring box from his pocket and looked at the ring one more time. He clapped it shut and tossed it up in the air then caught it. He put the ring box back into his pocket and set his jaw. One day he would put the ring on.

# ACKNOWLEDGEMENTS

First and foremost I would like to thank God for dropping this idea in my heart. Then secondly, this book wouldn't exist if it weren't for my friend Lena Sterley who tricked me into writing a novel. Thank you for reading the manuscript several times and always encouraging me to keep going. I also must thank my husband Parker who believed I could write a novel that people would actually want to purchase. Thank you for supporting this creative journey. Thank you to my daughter Izzy for listening to me read the novel out loud and being my cheerleader from the beginning. Thank you Grandma, Fern Deuchar, your surprise gift was the seed that took this to the next level and it meant the world to me that you invested into this book. Thank you to Fred and Pam Kropp, Shelly Kropp, Abi Farrington, Laura Roy, Melissa Lucia, Kristen Ryan, Nicole Moy, Fred and Hope Benthin for reading the drafts and giving me precious feedback. Thanks to Michelle Hsu for helping me find beta readers. Thank you to Jim Spivey for telling me that my first draft was actually three books. It was hard to swallow but that critical feedback made the story even better. Thank you to Dave Provolo for designing the cover and layout. Thank you to Kendall Ashley for giving me tremendous advice and gold stamping the novel with minor changes. Thank you to Lana Barnes for helping me with punctuation, grammar and not saying the same word over and over.

COMING SOON

SLINGSHOT

Book Two

The Kingston Chronicles

Find more at www.jcbenthin.com.

# ABOUT THE AUTHOR

J.C. Benthin has been writing since a young age winning a Father's Day essay contest with the Kansas City Star justifying "Why my Dad's the Best Outdoorsman" which won a John Deere lawnmower and a Webber grill. In college, a literary agent pursued the author for a collection of essays. Adulthood brought the opportunity to write stories for a next generation interactive publisher as well as an option on a screenplay by a Hollywood producer. The Kingston Chronicles initially began with a TV pilot titled "Three Zero" and expanded into a novel set ten years earlier. The author resides in Berkeley, California.

Made in the USA
Lexington, KY
31 August 2019